Thirty Days of Red

Geraldine Solon

Chartier Press

ISBN# 978-0692428603
Thirty Days of Red
Copyright ©2015 by Geraldine Solon
All rights reserved.

Cover Design: Natasha Brown

For my greatest treasures,
Arnel and Stefan

Prologue

I saw it coming and couldn't deny it. When the person you love collapses right in front of you with eyes flickering like strobe lights at a club, you know damn well you need to call for help. But I didn't. I just stood there, listening to the waves of air emerging from his chest, counting the seconds when he would go. But he stayed, and I was Olivia Walters once again, the nurse who took care of everyone except herself.

Day 1

Liv

My garage doesn't only store valuable tokens and trash. It stores secrets, stories only my husband and I know. Even so, today, I opened my home to strangers—to get rid of what we don't need and keep what's vital.

Counting the money from the sales, I examine David's medical bills piled on a container. This doesn't come close to what's due.

A whistle startles me.

I turn around and spot Christopher Harris, my best friend since senior year in high school. David would exude a frown if he saw him, often complaining I spent more time with Christopher than with him. I'm glad Christopher's here to comfort me.

He raises his eyebrows. "You need to get out of those scrubs."

That's Christopher, blunt like vomit.

"You know how comfy they are." I give him a big hug. "You're late for the party. The garage sale is over."

"Sorry." A puppy dog look appears on his face. Setting a spider web to the side, he sneezes, studies the boxes, and shakes his head. "Good lord, what do you have here?"

"Stuff we've accumulated over the years. Lots of junk, as you can witness."

My mother-in-law exits the back door and sets two glasses of lemonade on the table.

Christopher kisses both of her cheeks. "Diana, you're looking fabulous as ever."

My ever-jolly mother-in-law straightens her khaki dress and does a curtsy. "I thought I heard your voice. How are you, Christopher?"

"Never been better. Just got a massage. Which explains why I'm late." He smirks at me. "I feel like a new man."

"You're spoiled." She winks.

"Yup, Christopher is always ready for an adventure." I set folding chairs for us to sit.

We settle in our seats.

"Of course. I'm leaving for a Mediterranean cruise in a week and will need to eliminate this." He sucks in his abs.

My mother-in-law giggles. She pretends everything's all right despite her son recovering from a coma. David came home a month ago and since I'm a nurse, I opted to take care of David at home versus a facility so I can monitor him around the clock. My mother-in-law can be more of a handful compared to David. *She* is the attention seeker.

"I remember going on a cruise when I was your age. I had so much fun," she says.

As they continued to chatter, I dump trash in the garbage bin.

"Hey, Liv, I think you should join me," Christopher says.

I roll my eyes. "And who will provide for David's care?"

"Oh, I can do that," my mother-in-law chimes in.

Laughter erupts out of me. "Mom, you complained about leaving your cat alone."

"I can always bring Homer to stay with us." She shrugs and flashes me a sheepish grin.

"Did you forget David's allergic to cats?" I remind her.

"Right. Let me leave you both while I check on David." She scoots to the back door.

Facing Christopher, I say, "She doesn't realize the responsibility entailed to treating a sick person."

"But you can't be everybody's caretaker."

"I know. I know." Tears well. David had been so energetic, never failing to go on his morning run or hike on the weekends. I hate seeing him so helpless and not being able to remember a thing.

"What did the doctor say?"

After taking a sip of my lemonade, I swallow hard. Although David talks and has regained his strength, he seems to be lost in space. "There's no guarantee he'll regain his memory back."

"There has to be a break from all of this. Although the bills are piling up and work is calling you, we can do better than this garage sale. I can organize a fundraiser. You have to remember to take care of *you*." He squeezes my arms. "You're exhausted, drained, and hell, no sex."

Laughter spills from my mouth, but it's short lived. "Right."

"Girl, there must be cobwebs down there."

"Stop. C'mon, help me go through these boxes." Christopher manages to wipe out the gray shades in my life. I point to the remaining ones in the corner. "I don't want to be a dumb hoarder."

A grin forms his lips. "Okay. I'll work on these two small ones."

"Be sure to show me before you throw out anything."

He shakes his head. "You *are* a hoarder."

I open the box and scream as a spider crawls out. "Get rid of that."

"Is everything all right?" my mother-in-law calls from the kitchen. She's supposed to be upstairs with David and not eavesdropping on our conversation.

"Yes, just a spider."

We both giggle.

"My dear, your hands are full," Christopher says.

"Tell me about it."

He ransacks the remaining box and slits it open. Christopher removes an envelope and reads. "'Dear David...'"

"Hey, those are our love letters."

"'I was so touched...' I didn't know you were cheesy back during the day," he chides.

I pluck the card from his hands and return the items inside the box. "We were college sweethearts. Did you forget?"

Christopher bats his eyelashes. "You've been *sweethearts* for as long as I can recall."

My thoughts shift to the day David and I first met.

High heels clasped around my finger, I strode barefoot toward the door to my dorm. Tears trickled down my cheeks as I fumbled with my key.

"Excuse me," a male voice called out to me.

I refused to turn around after my date stood me up.

He appeared in front of me, green eyes spelled with gentleness. "I'm sorry, but my conscience will bother me if I didn't ask you why you're crying."

Not saying a word, I glared at him.

He raised his hands in the air. "I saw you waiting at the cafe and—"

"You've been following me," I cut him off.

"Yes, I mean, no... not the way you think." He dug his hand inside his pocket. "A beautiful lady like you shouldn't be sad. I want to cheer you up."

Our eyes locked, and from that day on, I knew David was a keeper.

Christopher snaps his fingers. "Hey, are you listening to me?"

"Huh? I'm sorry." I set the letters aside.

"I'm sure there's something you want to do for yourself, don't you?"

"Actually... I planned on starting a thirty-day wisdom project that should help me cope during this time of grief."

"Geez, so profound of you. Tell me more about it."

"I need to write down the things I learn each day for a compilation of thirty days."

He tucks a strand of my long strawberry blond hair behind my ears. "That sounds useful."

"Yeah. I envy you, my friend. I wish I could wake up in a different place every morning and feel alive again."

"Sweetie, you need to think about my invitation. Imagine you and I on a cruise. We'll have loads of fun and not to mention all the laughter."

I grin. "Let me take that box of love letters inside. Perhaps I can read it to David before I sleep."

As Christopher bids me goodbye, my shoulders drop knowing it will be another quiet night. I can't bear to look at David, who only gives me blank stares and converses with no emotions.

* * *

That evening, I cuddle David in bed as I comb his wispy brown hair.

Gathering the letters and cards, I inch beside him. "Honey, I found your letters to me in college. Remember our tagline? You'd always say, 'I love you first,' and I'd say, 'No, I loved you the minute I saw you', and you'd argue, 'But I saw you first.' We were inseparable." A giggle burst out, my emotions bittersweet.

David watches me and repeats. "Letters."

When I unfasten an envelope, a photo of David and I pop out.

Ignoring his lifeless expression, I add, "I remember this. We had a tennis match, and you were amazing." Leaning my head on his shoulder, I spot a notebook. "When we're old, we can read these letters again and show them to our children and grandchildren…"

For the past six years, I tried to get pregnant but failed. The doctors told us to be patient despite my three miscarriages. Perhaps children and grandchildren aren't in our future.

A notebook is inside the box. I recognize David's handwriting. It's written as if he was in hurry.

Thirty Days Before I Leave My Wife.

My hands freeze. Is this for real? I reread the note again. A cold shiver runs through my spine. Dashing to the toilet, I throw up the last piece of lasagna I ate that evening. Soaking my face with water, I start hyperventilating. *Why would David want to leave me? Shit, I was a good wife. I* am *a good wife.*

David lies in bed clueless and oblivious to the world while I inch back close to him. A part of me wants to smother him with a pillow, and another side of me wishes to ask him why.

Aware it's late; I grab my iPhone and text Christopher. *I'm coming with you on the cruise.*

Then I return all the letters including his notebook inside the box and seal it over and over and over again until the box is nothing but tape.

"Nobody can touch this box," I announce, slanting my eyes toward David to check if he would react. I tuck it underneath my clothes, inside our closet where it's safe and I can *forget*. Yes, that's right. *All I want to do is forget David is in a coma, forget the medical bills, forget David planned to leave me, and forget I'm Olivia Walters—David's wife.*

Day 2

Liv

My mother-in-law hugs me tight before Christopher and I board the plane to Barcelona. After seeing me pace around my bedroom like a caged animal, Diana insisted I go with Christopher. The caregiver and she would take turns in attending to David's needs while I'm away.

"Don't worry, I'll keep David safe," she whispers. Her words trigger a memory.

David's hands covered my eyes. "Just a few more steps and we'll be there."

A cold gust of wind brushed my cheeks. "Where are you taking me?"

He clasped my hand. "I want our first date to be special."

His smooth voice and the strong waves crashing to the shore crept inside my ears.

"We're here." David removed his hands, and right in front of me displayed a pink sky that cloaked the golden sun.

Silence crossed between us. The way he held my hand made me feel safe.

"Didn't I say I wanted to cheer you up?" He cupped my cheek, leaned forward, and rested his lips on mine.

Eyes closed, I didn't want this moment to end.

My mother-in-law releases me from her embrace. *Safe? Safe* is what I felt that day on the beach. *Safe* is what made me marry David. *Safe* is all I ever associated with him until I read the letter.

But I'm here to forget.

***

The flight from San Francisco to Barcelona is smooth, but I don't sleep a wink. The cruise line awaits us with her majestic presence. As I gaze at the mother ship, a surge of excitement washes upon me.

Christopher socializes with other patrons while clutching my arm. Should I tell him? He always thought David seemed too weak for me, that I carried him on my wing. I didn't know what he meant until we got married and I wore the pants. But Christopher said as long as I was happy, then that's all that mattered.

We head to our cabin and set our suitcases on the side. A sailor-themed room with two full-sized beds welcomes us.

Christopher sprawls himself on the bed overlooking the ocean. "La Dolce Vita."

Out the window, the sun continues to set, and I wish the sea can sweep away my memory and erase what I read.

Christopher sways his hips. "What do you want to do? Swim? We can sunbathe on the pool. Go bowling or gambling. You name it, Liv."

"How about I go to sleep?" I remove my shoes.

"Sleep?" He raises his eyebrows. "No, no, no. We are going to party, girl. We'll paint the town red."

I chuckle. Fun. Yes, that's the point of all of this. Seven days with nobody to think about but myself and not feel guilty about anything. Still, images of David's goal keep flashing through my head, making my mind spin. "I need a drink."

"That's my girl." Christopher claps his hands. "I promise you this will be a vacation of a lifetime." He unfastens the zipper of my luggage. "Let me choose your outfit." He removes two dresses— black and red. "I'll go with red." He presses his lips together. "Oh, boy. I better be your bodyguard tonight."

***

Red is the color of strength. Red is the color of blood. Red describes the fury inside me.

But tonight I'm going to drown myself in the Bloody Mary that I order.

While Christopher dances the night away, I sit by the bar with my legs crossed. From working as a nurse, I've learned to gauge people based on their actions. Pain delivers a threshold that's not tangible. Patients come to me needing reassurance more than cure, and most of the time, they seek someone they can trust.

Sipping my drink, I study the people swaying their bodies. Are they here to have fun? Are they high on some drug? Are they nursing a broken heart, or are they like me, wanting to forget?

Christopher points at me, requesting me to join him at the dance floor, but I shake my head.

Taking a big gulp of my Bloody Mary, I tell myself that tonight, I'm going to chill and be the outsider. I'm going to think about what would it be like to be someone else and not Olivia Walters.

A soft tap on my shoulder wisps me back to reality. Right before me is a tall man with dark wavy hair and the smoothest skin. He flashes me a dreamy look, like the one you see in the movies. His long-sleeve shirt doesn't hide his broad shoulders and chest.

With the music blasting in my ears, I lean forward. "I'm sorry. Can I help you?"

He runs his fingers through my hair and whispers, "Something tells me I can help you."

My throat constricts. Am I that obvious? How can he read through me? He intimidates me. His muscular scent mixed with fabric softener tugs me in the inside. "I'm not sure what to say."

"You don't have to say anything." He sits beside me.

Pressing my lips together, I admire his curly lashes and thick eyebrows. Why is he so beautiful?

"Are you alone?"

"With a friend." I search for Christopher, but he's lost in the crowd.

The man eyes my wedding ring. "Your husband?" When I don't respond, he adds, "You don't need to answer that."

This man is teasing me, and I don't know how to handle him. Do I look available?

He orders two drinks for both of us—Sangria for me and Scotch for him.

The alcohol consumes me. I stare at his long and hairy hands with clean fingernails, imagining how I would feel if he touched my *cherry*. Guilt washes upon me and I decide to push away those dirty thoughts.

We chat about the cruise and the destinations we'll be visiting and how he loves to cook, but he doesn't dare ask me again about myself.

Moments later, Christopher appears, all sweaty and panting. "Listen, dearie, I met some friends who are inviting me to hang out with them." He spots the man beside me and leans in close to whispers, "Who is he?"

I wave my hands in the air and shrug, pretending the man didn't exist.

"Okay." He smirks, eyeing him again. "Don't wait up for me."

"Have fun." When Christopher disappears, I face my drinking partner for the night.

"So, that's your friend."

"Yes." I gulp my drink and set it on the countertop. "And I think I better go."

"Wait." He caresses my arm. "I want to see you again."

My heart flutters. It's been a long time since a man looked at me with so much desire and passion.

Not waiting for me to answer, he says, "Meet me here tomorrow night. Same time."

I gaze at his deep-set eyes and rise from the bar stool. "I won't promise."

He pulls me toward his chest. I can smell his breath—Scotch mixed with lime—and almost want to taste his supple lips. "I'm Aiden."

"Please to meet you, Aiden." I extend my hand, fiery from the alcohol and his touch. "You can call me Red."

"Red?" He seems amused and doesn't let go of my hand. "Never met anyone by that name before."

I sling my purse around my shoulder and spring a few steps before turning back. "There's always a first time."

As I stride back to my cabin, ready to remove my high heels, I think about what I can add to my thirty-day wisdom project. Never underestimate the power of lust.

Red also stands for passion.

Day 3

Liv

Christopher doesn't stop blabbering about Patrick Deakin, the man he met last night. The dark circles in his eyes depict he had quite an adventure, which reminds me about the day David proposed.

A fog enveloped the sky. Hand in hand, David and I crossed the Golden Gate Bridge. His long fingers clasped against my tiny hand gave me a reason to feel safe.

Oatmeal-colored scarf wrapped around my neck, I zipped my coat. "Brrr, it's freezing. We should have picked another day to come here."

Although it had been two years since we dated, David was still full of surprises. We didn't have any money, but we had each other.

David squeezed my hand when we reached the center. "This is the perfect spot."

I raised my eyebrows. "For what?"

With one knee bent, David removed a small black box and opened it. "To the love of my life, when I'm with you, I feel six feet taller, I don't have to tell you what's on my mind since you already know and I don't have to look elsewhere as long as you're by my side. To the woman I want to spend the rest of my life with, will you marry me?"

Heart fluttering and dumbfounded, I burst into tears. "Oh, David, you always know how to put a smile on my face."

Hail cascaded down my cheeks, but all I felt was heat permeating inside me. I was going to now be David Walters' wife.

A smile played on his lips. "Is that a yes?" He took my hand and slipped the ring onto my finger.

"Yes."

The sun glaring from the sky morphs me back into reality.

Everything about Barcelona spells life. Together with hundreds of tourists, Christopher and I stroll *La Rambla,* the streets of Barcelona and soon find ourselves in the market, *La Boqueria.* A wide array of flowers, fruits, cheeses, and their famous legs of ham entice us. The scent of rawness captivates me the most and makes my mouth water.

Christopher ignores me while he admires attractive Spanish men.

I tug his arm. "Let's get out of here."

"Wait. I have every reason to stay," he pleads.

Moments later, we are seated at the Royal Plaza, *Placa Reial.*

I gaze at the open space. "This is a better place for people watching. You get a clearer view."

"I agree." Christopher winks.

"You need to be more discreet, you know." I dig in my *Zarzuela de Marisco* and moan as the garlic and olive oil melts in my mouth.

"No use hiding what you feel." He plunges a *Patata Brava* in his mouth.

After our late lunch, we explore the giant *Gothic Barcelona Cathedral.* From the outside, we witness street performers dancing as we walk alongside more cafes. Swans greet us in the courtyard.

"I read somewhere that the swans just settled in here," Christopher says.

"You seem to be up to date, my dear."

"Of course." He escorts me inside. "We're ahead of the game."

I avert my gaze to the high ceiling of Roman walls and gothic architecture pointing to the sky, struck by its grandness, as if transcending between time. Moments like this open a big part of me I haven't explored yet. Traveling to a new place only reminds me of the vastness of culture and how much we don't know. David promised to take me to Paris for my birthday, but after all these years; we never managed to leave the country.

We inch our way out of the Cathedral.

Christopher nudges his shoulder against mine. "I don't know about you, but my hair stood inside there."

"Were you admonished for your guilty pleasures?" I chide.

He pinches my arm as we stroll back to the ship. "So what are you doing tonight?"

"I suppose you and Patrick made plans."

Giggles erupt from his mouth. "Hope you don't mind. He asked me to see him after dinner."

My throat clears. "I don't want to deprive you of your needs." I explode into laughter.

"See? I told you this trip would be fun. Don't wait up for me." We board the cruise liner. After a sumptuous seafood buffet, Christopher drops me off in the cabin then rushes to meet Patrick. Glancing at my watch, I realize I have ten minutes to decide if I will meet Aiden. Should I?

Inside my suitcase, I spot a crimson scarf that would go well with my spaghetti strapped ebony dress.

After twirling the scarf around my neck, I put on a darker shade of scarlet lipstick and add a twist of shimmery gloss. I apply black mascara and perfume before exiting the cabin.

Aiden sits on the same stool, watching every step I take toward him. I draw in deep breaths. Upon my reaching him, he takes my hand and brings it to his lips, studying my face. He lays a kiss, soft like the clouds. "You came."

"I'm not a flake."

He raised his eyebrows. "We can try the *Burgundy Lounge*. It's not too noisy."

An internal struggle stops me in my tracks, but I remind myself I'm not Olivia. I'm *Red*. And Red is free to do anything she wants.

We spot scarlet velvet chairs and dim lights as we enter the lounge. A man with pin-stripes suite plays the piano.

Aiden gestures for me to sit down and rests beside me. "What would you like to order?"

I study the menu remembering what he ordered for me last night. "I'd love a Sangria."

The waiter approaches, and he orders one for me and Scotch on the rocks with lime for him.

"That seems to be your signature drink," I comment.

His eyes sweep down where my legs are crossed then back at me. "I like my drinks to be bracing like the winter." He presses his lips together. "But food should always be moist like your lips."

At a loss for words, I lean backward but can't help licking my lips.

The waiter serves our drinks. A woman whose white dress clings to her slender frame as she approaches the stage welcomes everyone before delivering a love song.

Aiden inches closer to me. He caresses my hand and sends shivers down my spine. How long has it been since David caressed my hand? My memory fails me. I know this is wrong, but I continue to keep still while I drink.

He removes the orange from my glass and traces it on my lips. Heart throbbing, I nibble on a piece, but he pulls it away, popping it in his mouth and chews. Eyes wide open, he reaches for my neck and mumbles in a hushed tone, "I stole your Vitamin C."

My body freezes. "That's okay. I can share."

We order more drinks as the lady sings a set of songs.

Although my mind nudges me to go back to my cabin, my body feels like Velcro glued to the seat. The crowd begins to fade until only a few couples remain.

After paying the tab, Aiden draws in a breath. "I heard this is the best time to be on the deck." He fingers my scarf, and I find myself walking alongside him.

Silence crosses between us upon reaching the deck. A gust of wind sweeps my hair when we face the ocean. The sight of water calms me.

Aiden inches near me and plucks my scarf, gently tying my arms behind. "You're my prisoner now." His tongue probes my ears.

I narrow my gaze toward him, but I can't find my voice. My inner muse is telling me to run, but the alcohol has taken the better part of me, inducing me to stay. Recalling David's plan to leave, I find myself more drawn to Aiden.

He cups my face with both hands and caresses my lips with his. Eyes shut, I stroke his tongue against mine, tasting the Scotch and lime and the softness of his lips. His tongue cascades down my neck, and I moan.

Aiden traces his finger down my bare arm. I shake, wanting to hold him close and feel the intimacy David and I once shared. Continuing to kiss me, he tugs my arm and guides me to his cabin. When we arrive, he undresses me with his mouth, lays me down the bed and rips my dress. I want to feel his tongue again.

I don't know what the hell I'm doing, but I feel alive.

My cherry pulsates down there. He removes my scarf, and it's my turn to stroke his back. My hands slides down his buttocks, pulling him inside me.

I want him. I need him. I have to have him. When was the last time David and I had sex? Mind-blowing sex?

My memory shifted to after we got married, when David and I bought our first condominium. We were lucky to get a good price, but later discovered the heater wasn't working.

All we had was a mattress, but we didn't care as long as we had each other.

"I feel cold." I pulled the comforter closer to my chin.

"You know the solution to that." He cupped my face, gazing into my eyes like I was the most important woman in the world.

"That's a temporary fix." I bit his chin as his hands groped me down there.

We spent the whole day in bed, not worrying about any responsibilities, thrilled to be glued to each other. We were young, carefree and very much in love.

But now I'm awaken by Aiden, who teases me and licks my cherry while fondling my breasts. My body moves up and down, following the rhythm of his tongue. Right when I'm about to explode, he thrusts inside me and presses his moist lips on my mouth. I can taste myself. I savor him… both of us.

Heat emanates while he grinds. Pulling my legs up, he continues to rock forward and back. I drink his musky scent, combined with sweat. Intoxicated by lust, I want more.

My thighs shake, and I reach to the edge of the bed while I release. He's still going on, and I'm still stimulated. With one hand cupped on my breast, he pulls me on top of him and clings to my thighs as I rock my body to and fro.

His breathing is ragged, and this time, I want to please him. I continue to hop up and down until we both explode in ecstasy.

We share a tight embrace before I collapse beside him and lean on his arm. He traces my nipples then snakes his arms around my waist.

While Aiden drifts off to sleep, I curl close to him, smoothing away wisps of his hair. He looks so peaceful, like a baby. I almost want to sing a lullaby. Moments later, I let go from his embrace and rise out of the bed. Christopher might be looking for me and I should get back. Tiptoeing, I slip into my dress, carrying my heels and purse, and exit the door.

Upon arrival to my cabin, I insert the key and try to be as quiet as I can. I spot the empty beds and no sign of Christopher. "Phew." I sigh in relief then hop into my pajamas.

In bed, I replay what happened earlier, but my delight turns into rage as I curl my hand into a fist. Am I naive to overlook David's intentions of putting an end to our marriage? Slamming my hand into the wall, I realize trust is not one of my best suits. I trusted my husband, never anticipating he planned to leave me. And now I allowed myself to be intimate with a stranger not thinking about the consequences of my actions. Then, I tell myself I'm not Olivia Walters. A smile spreads across my lips. *I'm Red.*

Day 4

Liv

Christopher is clueless I had a wild night that evening. All he talks about is how special Patrick made him feel by giving him a nice tie.

I continue to nod as I gaze at the paintings in the *Picasso* museum, thankful we have another day in vibrant Barcelona.

"You look different," Christopher says.

Resting my hand on my cheek, I say, "Perhaps it's the Spanish air."

He shrugs. "You appear to be well rested."

If only he knew.

A knot forms in my stomach, and my thoughts shift to the day I tasted despair after losing my baby.

"I have the keys," David called out from the kitchen.

"Give me a few minutes." I applied lipstick. Following him to the car, I hummed. "We're going to be parents."

Backing up from the driveway, David beamed from side to side. "Can you imagine a mini me or mini you?"

"Remember. I want it to be a surprise. Don't try asking the doctor what the sex is."

"Promise." He stepped on the gas. "You also need to promise me one thing?"

"What?" I faced him.

"If the baby's a girl, she'll only be allowed to date when she's eighteen."

Eyebrows raised, I laughed. "Boy, our daughter's going to have a guard dog. She won't need one if she's feisty like me."

He squeezed my hand. "And if it's a boy, I'll teach him to protect his mommy."

My heart melted. "You're going to be a great dad, David."

David brought my hand to his lips and kissed it.

"I'd like to name her Zoe if she's a girl," I said.

"Zoe sounds nice. And if he's a boy?"

Lips pressed together, I grin. "I don't know, something tells me we're having a girl."

Our eyes locked and knowing we were both going to be parents, made me love him more.

What started out as an exciting day soon turned sour shortly after we arrived at the doctor's office.

Eager to expose my bump, I lied down as Dr. McGregor applied gel on my belly. "I've been taking my vitamins, eating healthy, and reading aloud."

Eyes glued to the screen, he nods. "That's good."

"I made sure Liv cut out her caffeine," David added.

Dr. McGregor didn't flinch.

I sensed something was wrong. "Dr. McGregor?"

Lips formed in a straight line, he faced me. "I'm sorry..."

Those simple words struck me like a bomb. *I would never be a mother.*

Similar to the abstract paintings displayed on the wall, nothing made sense that day. A part of me wants to get lost in the artwork, and run away from my complicated life.

Christopher pokes me back to reality. "I'm sorry if I stayed out late last night."

"Don't worry about it. I don't expect you to be with me twenty-four seven."

After visiting the museum, we take a tour of the *Gothic Quarter*, the old town of Barcelona. I admire the ancient, towering architecture, and as we end our day with a good old *Café Solo*, I learn something about myself in the two days of my stay in Barcelona. Life is about perspective. *I could be home grieving about my husband's condition and his plan to break our marriage, or I could be here, embracing life, knowing that tomorrow I'll be waking up in Toulon, France.*

***

Christopher and I try a formal restaurant that evening. As he munches on his *Gambas*, I ask him, "Are you seeing Patrick tonight?"

"He wants to go gambling."

"Cool."

"I feel guilty about leaving you behind. Why don't you join us?"

"Me?" I rest my fingers on my chest. "I don't gamble."

"You can always hang out with us. C'mon." He wipes his mouth with a napkin.

"I'm quite exhausted with all the walking today." I yawn.

"Okay."

"Sorry. I need all of my energy for tomorrow."

"*Oui.*"

After dinner, Christopher drops me off the cabin and disappears into the night.

Leaning my head on the door, I contemplate if I should see Aiden or stay home. Nothing about tonight feels right. It's a choice between conscience and compulsion, and I choose the latter.

"Screw it."

My heart pounding, I reach Aiden's cabin. Everything about Aiden spells danger, but I'm tired of doing the right thing and being the good wife. Tonight, I will quench my thirst of lust.

I knock lightly, press my ears against the door, and hear faint music. Maybe he's with someone else, but I can't help knocking again.

Nothing.

When I'm ready to leave, the door flings open and Aiden appears with a towel wrapped around his waist. His body is glowing with beads of water while he stares at me from head to toe.

"Did you come back for this?" He pulls out my red silk scarf from the table behind him. I never realized it was missing.

"No." I press my body against his. "I came for *you.*"

Our lips touch, and he turns me around in a swirl, carrying me to the bathroom.

I slide down the zipper of my dress and toss my sandals to the side. Together, we soak inside the bathtub. My back leaning against his chest, I allow him to massage my breasts with suds. He presses his crotch from behind and bends down to caress the soap on my legs.

Hair twirled in a bow, I massage my neck on his stubble chin and moan. Underneath my cherry, he presses his finger inside. My breathing becomes more rapid while I rub the shaft of his crotch. He sticks two fingers inside, pulls them out, and licks them.

I pick up the champagne glass on the marble floor and take a sip. He kisses me, continuing to fondle me down there. When we rinse and towel off, Aiden carries me and places me on top of the counter. He pushes inside me and clasps my body.

"Did you miss me?"

"Yes," I moan.

"Tell me you want this every day," he grunts.

"I want this *every day*."

Hands wrapped around my waist, he bends me forward while he continues to rock me.

I can feel him, taste him, breathe him.

Spanking my buttocks, he releases me so I can face and kiss him.

Moments later, we lie in bed, and I watch him sleep. *I don't know how long this will last, but one thing I learned today is that acting on my compulsion is worth it.*

Day 5

Liv

Today is our fourth day of the cruise, and I'm getting used to waking up every morning in a different place. With our navy blue shirts and white shorts, Christopher and I step out of the liner, welcoming the breeze and ready to venture in the heart of Toulon, France.

"*Bonjour, mademoiselle.*" Christopher puts on his bad French accent.

I roll my eyes and clamp my hand on my straw hat to keep it from flying away. We explore the old town and market.

"Do we look too touristy?" Christopher strides by the monuments.

"We *are* tourists. Nothing wrong with that."

Hips swayed, he muses, "I just want to blend with the crowd."

"You're my evil sailor twin," I chide.

"What would you do without me?" He winks.

We walk a few distances to the beach. I lie out our towel and remove my top.

"You sure love the color red, don't you?" Christopher eyes my bikini.

Applying sunscreen on my thighs, I shrug. "I didn't realize what I packed. It was a last minute decision, remember?"

Christopher removes his shirt and sprays sunscreen on his arms and chest. "I never got to ask you why you decided to come."

I'm not ready to disclose any information about Aiden or David's plan to leave me. "Like you said, I can't keep taking care of everybody."

"Glad you came." He lies down beside me. "And I hope David is okay."

"He's fine, I called earlier today and spoke to Mom. David was asleep."

The sun feels as if it's melting my chest as I close my eyes. Thoughts of Aiden creep inside my mind. I'm so excited to see him tonight. I wonder what he does all day. Is he touring the streets like Christopher and I? There's not much I know about him, but it's better that way. *Life shouldn't be complicated. Today, I'm going to embrace the present.*

***

Back at our cabin, Christopher gathers the magnets and key chains he bought for his sister from the places we visited and packs them inside his suitcase. Not knowing what else to get them, I bought David and my mother-in-law shirts from each stop.

"Is your relationship with Patrick serious?" I ask.

He flashes me a smile. "He wants me to meet his parents when we get back."

I cross my legs. "How much do you know about him?"

"Enough. He's a math teacher. I'm a financial analyst. Ain't that a match made in heaven?" He winks.

"Yes, but there's more to that. You never visited his place. He could be messy, or what if he's bipolar?"

Christopher bursts out laughter. "Boy, you have a wild imagination. I'm not marrying him."

"I don't want you to get hurt."

"And I don't want to end up alone. Life is about risks, and I need to try." He catches a glimpse of his watch. "I gotta meet Patrick at the casino."

"A gambler. Now that's one of his vices." I shake my finger.

"Oh, stop it." He kisses me goodbye on both cheeks and heads for the door.

My feet ran after him. "Wait."

Christopher turns back. "Did I forget something?"

High heels in hand, I say, "It's time I met Patrick."

***

The three of us are playing on the slot machines and enjoying cocktails. Patrick and Christopher look giddy when they giggle. Their eyes twinkle each time one wins a point, and their bodies seem to be in tune. Patrick glances at me as if he wants my approval.

Christopher puts his arms around me. "Liv here has been my best friend since high school. I call her my evil twin," he rambles, "even though she's the opposite of evil. She keeps me grounded."

I roll my eyes. Christopher is unaware about what transpired with Aiden.

"It pays to have a friend like Liv," Patrick says.

The clock strikes midnight and my winning streak fades. My hormones now raging for Aiden, and Christopher and Patrick are holding hands.

"Lovebirds, I'm going to excuse myself before I snooze."

"What are you, Cinderella?" Christopher chides.

"I need my beauty sleep."

We group hug.

The cruise is more vibrant at night, but there's only one person who will complete my evening.

Hoping he's awake, I knock slightly upon reaching his cabin.

The door opens, and Aiden stands there, a white terry robe covering his lean body. "I thought you'd never come." He slides his finger down my chest and grabs me inside.

"What's that smell?" I remove my heels and toss my hair to the side, inhaling the lemongrass scent.

"Risotto, courtesy of the chef." He reaches for a fork and feeds me.

I moan in delight.

"I'm thrilled you love it." He settles me in a chair while he prepares a plate for me.

We eat in silence, gazing into each other's eyes. A thought of David pops in my mind and I'm not sure when our passion ended.

"I'm late for work." I rushed down the steps.

"Why can't you even look at me?" David yelled.

I stormed out of the house. David and I had dreams of raising a family. How could I tell him he was a reminder of the failure I was for not being able to provide him with a child?

Aiden grabs me gently to the bed, taking me back into reality. The past few days with him allowed me to escape the situation back home. He pulls my red scarf and blindfolds me. "Let's play a game."

Licking my lips, I agree, hungry for a surprise.

"Let's say you're blind, you have no hands, and you're under the mercy of your master. All you can do is hear, smell, and taste."

"Yes, master."

He rubs a pebble-like object on my lips. "Tell me what this is."

I taste the salt and munch. "Almond?"

"Good guess."

Aiden's breath nuzzles the back of my neck. I draw in air as he traces my lips with what feels like cold strawberries. When I attempt to suck it, he pulls away. Instead he presses his lips against mine and pushes bits of strawberries into my mouth. My tongue caresses his, and I swallow the fruit.

"Do you like it?" He kisses me.

"Yes."

He undresses me and whispers, "I want a more exciting game."

A sharp object rests on my neck. My body stiffens. "Aiden, I'm not sure what kind of game you want to play."

He rotates me forward and handcuffs my arms. "You've been a very bad girl."

It barely hurts my skin, but my heart pounds and I explode into a cold sweat. What is he doing?

"Any last words?" He pulls my hair gently.

"Aiden, this isn't funny."

He massages my thighs, but I lie on my bare stomach, frozen. If I scream, who would come after me? Not even Christopher knows where I am.

The sheets rustle like fallen leaves. Aiden removes my handcuff and blindfold then pulls me to his chest. "I'm sorry. Did I scare you?"

Tears welling, I pick up my clothes and rise from the bed. "I need to go."

"But you just got here. I'm sorry. I wanted some fun."

Without hesitation, I slip into my dress and approach the door. "This was a mistake."

"Red, calm down." He approaches me.

Taking a step back, I straighten my shoulders. "I barely know you, and you don't have the faintest clue about me."

Caressing my cheek, he gazes into my eyes. "I'm aware you're a good kisser, and you point your toes when you're about to explode into an orgasm."

I try to keep a straight face.

Aiden fondles me down there, and my breathing grows ragged and my body freezes. I have allowed myself to fall under his spell. "You can't resist me even if you tried."

Why did he have to be so right?

"Okay." Aiden raises his hands in the air, as if he's resting his case. "I promise I won't touch you. Just stay with me tonight." He gestures to the table. "There's a lot of food."

I grab my heels, but stop.

"Please," he begs. "I'm not one to break a pledge."

I finally give in and perch on the chair. Aiden arranges another plate for me. We eat in silence like two coeds on the first day of school. When it's time for me to go, he brushes his lips against my cheek. I can't deny I want more.

"How did it feel being helpless?"

"I'm not *helpless*." I straighten my shoulders.

"You try not to be." He strokes my hair. "Yet you panicked when I tied you up and—"

"What do you expect? You're a stranger."

"A *stranger*?" He grins. "Each time I ask you about something, you put a wall between us. I don't want to hurt you. I'm here to rescue you."

Deep in thought, I stride back to my cabin. He seems to understand me more than David. *Will I ever feel safe again?*

Day 6

Liv

Christopher and I stroll the streets of Rome as I indulge in my tiramisu gelato. We stop at the *The Fontana di Trevi* where hundreds of tourists gather together.

Digging in his pocket, Christopher removes a penny and closes his eyes. I admire the three Roman god statues—Ocean, Abundance, and Health with their chariot horses. A huge part of me wishes to dive in the fountain and pretend I never existed. Another side of me wants to run away with Aiden and leave the past behind.

Maybe I should and just embrace my new identity—Red. What could be worse than being with David who doesn't remember anything about me or our life while I suffer each day, knowing he would have ended our marriage? What is there to come back to when all that's left are bittersweet memories?

Christopher nudges me. "Did you make a wish?"

I shake my head.

He furrows his eyebrows. "Legend states that if you throw a coin and make a wish, you'll return to Rome."

"Really? I don't believe in wishes. " I take a bigger scoop of my gelato and march toward the next stop.

"No harm in trying," he says.

Christopher and I explore the Sistine chapel, the Vatican, and climb the Spanish steps.

"Hey, Liv, I can tell you're sad since it's our last night, but didn't you enjoy yourself?"

"Of course I did." I tear up. "I'm not sure I'll be able to do this again."

"Yes, you will. You might want to take David with you."

David? How can I face him?

At a souvenir shop, Christopher haggles with the vendor while I pluck a miniature Leaning Tower of Pisa. My eyes moisten as I put on my sunglasses then wrap my hair in a bun.

Tomorrow morning, we'll dock and fly back to San Francisco. I don't want to leave. I only want to see Aiden and tell him how special he makes me feel. When I'm with him, I feel alive. Something I missed for a long time.

Souvenirs for David and my mother-in-law are now paid.

Voices of a couple arguing in Italian capture my attention. The woman raises her voice when I gaze in their direction. My heart stops as I spot the man with her. *Aiden*. They're both oblivious I'm there. The woman continues to comb her long auburn wavy hair. She points a finger at him while he darts back with strong words.

"You ready?" Christopher pokes me.

I glance back at the couple locked in a tight embrace.

My heart rips open like a dagger has been plunged into it.

He snaps his fingers. "Are you okay? Do you know them?"

"No." I shrug, taking a step forward. "We should go."

We stride back to the cruise.

"You seem quite edgy today."

"Let's not talk about that." I walk ahead of him toward our cabin. Once there, I pack my clothes and position my suitcase in the corner. "Are you seeing Patrick tonight?"

"I told Patrick I was worried about you and I should spend time with you before we head back." He folds his arms.

"Silly. Go see Patrick."

"And leave you alone here?" He unzips his luggage.

"I can go to the spa, get a massage. Read my book and savor some alone time." I bite my lip.

"If you say so."

"Christopher…" I give him a tight embrace. "Thank you."

"No point in being all mushy."

When he leaves, an image of the woman earlier that day dawns upon me. I need to find out who she is.

Slipping on a crimson shirt and jeans, I ask myself, am I ready to take the plunge with Aiden and leave everything behind? The idea sounds tempting, but I'm going to give myself one more night to think about it. If this will be my last night of being *Red*, I better enjoy it.

✳✳✳

Aiden's white shirt clings to his sculpted body. He welcomes me inside with a boyish grin.

"Where is she?" I search the cabin.

"Who?"

"The woman you were with earlier today."

He closes the door. "You were spying on me?"

"I wasn't *spying*. You both marched in front of me like I didn't exist. I never knew you spoke Italian."

"Let's be clear about one thing, Red." He gestures his hands in the air. "Don't try psychological profiling me. You think I'm not aware you're married? I bet your husband was having an affair, and you're here to forget."

I plop into a chair and begin to weep.

Aiden rushes to my side and comforts me. "Please don't cry. I'm on your side."

Sobbing some more, I'm at a loss of words. My emotions are like a roller coaster. I don't want to go home. How can I return when there's nothing left for me except taking care of David? Who will take care of me?

After removing his wallet from his back pocket, Aiden shows me a picture of the woman and him. The photo appears to be taken a decade ago from his more angular face. "She's my sister who lives in Rome. We were arguing about who will watch my aging father and my condition."

"Is there anything wrong with you?"

He slants his gaze to the floor. "I have renal failure."

"What! That's insane."

"Don't worry," he pacifies me. "I don't feel anything, and the doctor said I'm one of the lucky few who is healthy and asymptomatic."

I study him. He doesn't look like someone who has renal failure, but again I can't bear the thought of his condition worsening.

"Let's not talk about this. I want to focus on you."

Tears stain my cheeks. I'm thrilled Aiden shared a piece of him with me. I should do the same. In respect to change the subject, I say, "I didn't think you were Italian."

"Both of my parents were, which explains my passion for food."

I nod. "Are you going to take him in?"

He sighs. "Dad and I would never see eye to eye. We're both bullheaded, and he can be demanding at times."

"What do you plan to do?"

He shrugs.

My thoughts shift to my mother-in-law. She's both needy and stubborn, but thanks to her, I ventured on this cruise. "That's a major decision."

"What do you say we get some milkshakes and go bowling? I'm in the mood to do something fun." His warm hand grasps mine.

He never lets go while we march to the bowling alley, and I dream of knowing more about him. Aiden seems exciting, adventurous, reminding me of how David used to be.

We play a set of games, and Aiden tries to win the overachiever in me. With a straight set of strikes, I end up beating him by a few points.

He pokes me in the ribs. "You're a tough cookie."

"I thrive."

As we head back to his cabin, he pulls me close and smells my hair. "Remember what I told you when we met?"

I raise my eyebrows.

"That I might be able to help you? Looks like you're going through something deep."

If I tell him, I'll lose a part of myself and it'll only complicate my life even more.

"Run away with me."

"What?" Temptation tugs in my intestines.

"You're halfway there. You have a choice to either move forward or go back."

I picture the headlines—Recovering coma patient's wife disappears after embarking on a Mediterranean cruise. The thought sounds inviting, but cheating on David doesn't change how much I love him. I don't want to think of the consequences so I press my finger against his mouth. "I want to focus on tonight."

We enter his cabin. He carries me to the bed, undressing me with soft kisses. Under the dim lights, I close my eyes and allow him to take away my painful reality while he gently makes love to me.

Aiden looks at me straight in the eye. "Red, I'm giving you a chance of a lifetime. Meet me at the deck where we first kissed fifteen minutes before the ship docks. We can start a new life together."

I don't answer. *I want to remember this night forever, to cling to it as much as I can, to hold on to what I can hope for, because tomorrow, it will be all lost like a shattered vase.*

Day 1

David

Six days before the coma.

Liv bids me goodbye from downstairs. I'm still spaced out from the strong cold medicine I took last night. She's her usual self, writing down lists and ordering me what to do. She's acting like the superwoman she believes she is, thinking ahead and beyond, which leaves me left out since I'm the spur of the moment kind of guy who goes with the flow. My wife thinks she knows everything, but she has yet to figure out the surprise I have for her.

I'm tired of being known as *Liv's husband.* Even the Asian vendor at the farmer's market down the street where I buy my fresh vegetables never seems to remember my name. She often rubs her chin and says in her broken English, "Oh, yes, you Liv's husband."

I'm sick of it! Just because I'm a freelance graphic designer who works from home in my boxers doesn't mean my job ain't legitimate. My poor wife needs to prove to everyone what a good caretaker she is. The dark circles underneath her eyes reveal she barely gets any sleep from her swing shift job, and when she comes home, she cooks and cleans before going to bed.

I tried cooking and doing the chores for her, but she complains the food tastes bland or I poured too much bleach on the laundry. Nothing I do seems right.

No matter how I convince her she can't do it all, Liv shrugs and stares at me like I'm some kind of loser as she opens her journal. That stupid journal is empty inside, a long term-plan according to her, some thirty-day wisdom project.

Guess what, Liv. I'm also going to work on a thirty-day goal project.

I miss the bold and beautiful Olivia Walters I met in college. Although Liv always spoke her mind, she made me feel like I was the most important person in the world. My thoughts shift to my first birthday spent with Liv.

"Now it's my turn to surprise you," Liv whispered. "No cheating. Keep your eyes shut."

"Okay, but you know how impatient I am." I forced myself to keep still.

She counted to three. "Open your eyes."

Right in front of me was a rich-filled chocolate cake, balloons, and a wrapped gift, but the best part was Liv singing to me naked.

I grabbed her from behind and squeezed her.

She tickled me. "Not till you open your gift and take a bite of the cake."

"You baked this?"

"From scratch."

"Gosh. You never cease to surprise me." I tore off the wrapper and opened the box.

"And you thought you were the one with *surprises*." She winked.

Eying the watch, I pulled her toward me and kissed her neck. Her gift wasn't fancy, but I knew she had saved up her money to buy it for me, That's all that mattered. "Thank you for making my birthday special."

I never took the watch off my wrist. I slept with it and guarded it with my life.

I don't remember when I decided to stop wearing it. Perhaps it was when independence took over and the stronger she became, the less likely I existed.

A pen calls to me. I remove a notebook from inside my desk and scribble inside, *Thirty Days Before I Leave My Wife.*

Day 2

David

Five days before the coma.

Today's my birthday. Thirty-five years old. As I stir my green tea in the kitchen, I check to see if there are any voicemails on the phone. *Nada.* Not even a card or note from my wife. Did she forget?

I circle to my office, the only room my wife never enters. She can't stand the mess of Post-its scattered around my desk. The one time she came here was when I showed her the logo I created for the cousin of her best friend six months ago. Eyebrows raised, she seemed more concerned about the empty beer bottles lined up on the tray beside my desk, not to mention the futon bed I often take naps on.

"How can you work like this?" She coughed in disgust, not once complimenting me for the piece of work I did.

Turning on my computer, I check to see if my beloved wife emailed me. Disappointment stabs me on the inside. How could Liv forget? Liv the organizer! Liv the perfectionist! I glance at our photo with the dolphins.

I could still feel Liv's smooth skin against my face on our honeymoon in Hawaii. Our bodies glued on a hammock, I traced my finger down Liv's hips.

"When the honeymoon is over, are you going to leave me?" Liv asked.

"How can you say such a thing?"

She shrugged. "I might get fat, my breasts will sag, and you won't want me anymore."

I embraced her tight. "That will never happen."

"You promise?"

"Promise."

Where did all that love go?

"Shit!" I jab the letter opener on my desk. If she doesn't care about me, then maybe I should just go ahead with my plan and leave her.

***

Later that evening, Liv and I are eating opposite our four-seater dining table. She sips on her Bordeaux wine, her green eyes glued to a book, blond hair tied in a bun. I'm chewing leftover pot roast from the night before. God knows how much I hate pot roast. Damn it! Couldn't she even make this day special for me? Engrossed in reading her suspense novel, Liv hasn't even said one word to me, not even a blink or a smile. *Bitch!*

"I'm not hungry." I toss the plate aside, hoping she'd give me some attention.

She scans the table and nods.

After picking up the plate, I head to the kitchen and leave it on the dishwasher. I stride to the door and grab my jacket. "I'm going for a walk."

She approaches me as our eight-year-old gray Persian cat, Wilma, trails behind her. "Can you buy some cat litter?"

My heart sinks, but I pose a fake smile. "Sure." I want to blurt out that I can also purchase some rat poison.

"Thanks." She scoops Wilma in her arms and kisses her nose. "And please make sure you wipe your shoes before coming in. Mud sticks to the carpet."

I roll my eyes. "Will make a note of that."

Eager to leave, I march the streets of San Francisco. Perhaps I can do something nice for myself. It's my birthday. I need to get laid. When was the last time we had hot, raw sex? I rub my eyes. Liv and I are like old boring couples going through the routine of life. We don't have kids, and we basically live different lives.

After perusing the various bars in the city, I step inside Skyline. Dim lights, drunk sexy women, and lots of booze greet me. A lady dressed in a bikini dances on a pole up on the stage while people cheer for her.

"Hello, cowboy." A woman tucks a strand of brunette hair around her ear. Her full lips curl into a smile, her tank top and jeans so tight on her body.

Her friend clutches her arm around me. "What's a handsome man like you doing alone?"

I grin, perching on a bar stool while they both sit down beside me.

The bartender eyes me.

Raising a nod, I order, "I'll have a Budweiser."

"So, what's your name?" The brunette traces my jaw. "I've never seen you here before."

A group of rowdy men continue to cheer for the lady dancing.

My chin needs a good shave. "I happened to be in the area."

"I figured." She inches close to me, pressing her breasts against mine. "I'm Emily."

We shake hands. "David."

Her friend winks and leaves us alone.

Emily pulls my hand and takes me to the back dressing room where there are mirrors, makeup, and wigs displayed.

"Wait," I say.

"Sh!" She locks the door and whispers, "Don't worry. I own this place."

An erection arises as she removes my jacket and kisses me on the lips. She's so hot and well endowed and totally wants me, unlike Liv who doesn't give a shit about me.

Eyes shut, I allow her to undress me while I fondle her tits. Gosh, I've forgotten how breasts felt. I caress her and she strips naked and reaches for my belt. A part of me can't believe this is happening, but I pull my pants down. Lost in my tracks, I realize I didn't bring a condom, but as if on cue, she digs inside her purse and hands me one.

Body tilted, I raise her on top of the counter. She spreads her legs, welcoming me inside her like a king entering his palace. *Happy Birthday!* A song plays in my mind. I deserve this.

She moans in my ear. "I want it rough."

"Yes, baby. I'll show you what *rough* is." Against the wall, I slam inside her, my frolicking hands caressing her huge, juicy breasts in delight.

A loud knock interrupts our activity.

"Shit!" I pull away from her.

"In a minute," she shouts then grabs me back inside her.

I close my eyes, fear and a combination of adrenaline crawling upon me, but it's my birthday and I'm going to enjoy myself.

We savor the moment, lingering until we both release in ecstasy.

Emily tosses me my clothes before she quickly slips into her jeans and tank top. She leans close and wipes the lipstick of my lips. "I had fun."

I break into a smile. "You made my day."

Beads of sweat drip down my nape as I head back to the bar. Emily joins her friend and pretends nothing happened. I continue to drink, my eyes glued to another stripper dancing on the pole. *Did I just have sex?*

An hour has passed since I left, and I still need to buy the cat litter.

Emily is out of sight, but I wish I could say goodbye and thank her for a special night. Instead, I put on my jacket, exit the bar, and walk a few blocks to the twenty-four hour convenient store.

My shoulders slump when I reach the front driveway to our Victorian home. The lights are out. Liv's probably asleep, but I don't care. *I got laid.*

Unlocking the door, I step inside. Silence beckons me the minute I enter, not forgetting to wipe my shoes per Liv's request. I can swear I hear a whimper.

When I inch closer, the lights flash open and people shout surprise.

My jaw drops. The living room is filled with gifts and balloons.

Liv approaches me with a birthday cake with candles. "What took you so long?"

Sweat continues to pour down my neck. I'm speechless. Everyone sings happy birthday while I set the cat liter aside. I hang my jacket on the coat rack.

Liv reminds me to make a wish.

Guilt washes upon me. Suddenly, I'm the center of attention while my wife mingles with the other guests.

Stealing a glance, I wonder how she pulled this off. Did she do this because she loves me or to show off to her friends what a good wife she is? She fooled me again, proving to everyone else what a good wife she is. I make a mental note. *Goal One: Be ahead of the game.*

Day 3

David

Four days before the coma.

Light spills inside our bedroom. I'm still bedazzled from what happened the night before. Reaching out to the opposite side of the bed, I hope my wife and I can share a morning after rendezvous, but she's gone to work and I'm all alone to collect my thoughts. *Well, not really.* I remember the lazy Sundays we'd share in bed playing footsies and how Liv would just stare into my eyes like I was the only one that existed.

Wilma jumps into my bed and goes under the sheets, locking her tail in between my toes. Maybe she's aware of how I feel, deserted and lonely. But, hey, I got laid.

I push down the comforter and rise out of bed. What's today going to be like? Checking a few emails on the phone, I decide not to work. Perhaps I can continue celebrating.

***

A stroll along the streets of San Francisco without a schedule can be so liberating. The cool breeze uplifts my spirit. I'm free to indulge in whatever makes me happy.

I spot an old gentleman playing chess. One man keeps his gaze steady on the queen, while the man seated opposite from him rubs his chin, deliberating his next move.

That's it! I'm going to treat this like a game of chess until I kill the queen.

I march down the road and enter my favorite gelato shop.

The owner, Roberto, greets me with his jolly cheer. "We carry new flavors."

"Indulge me." I slant my gaze to the selections displayed. My mouth waters. I didn't eat breakfast.

Roberto takes a spoon, scoops dark chocolate ice cream, and passes the cup to me. "*Cioccolato con Peperoncino.* Hot-pepper infused dark chocolate." He winks.

"I love it. Anything to spice up my day."

Liv's words from two weeks ago come back to me. "You shouldn't consume chocolate ice cream in the morning. It'll ruin your digestion and leave you with a tummy ache."

My mouth waters. "Make that a double scoop."

Roberto grins as he fills the cup. "Glad you like it."

I'm in ecstasy. Acting like a rebellious teenager, I lick the spoon and moan. "Oh, Liv, if only you can see me now."

People trot down the street—couples holding hands, women walking their dogs, men rushing to cross the street. As I stand across Skyline bar, thoughts of Emily arouse me. The sign says they're closed, but I knock anyway.

The door opens, and a young lady with a ponytail wearing a gray hooded jacket and jeans pops outside. "We're closed."

I stare at her. "Thought I'd try."

"Hey, it's you."

Finger pointed to my chest, I ask, "Me?"

"It's Emily, remember?"

This lady seems a decade younger than the woman I had sex with last night.

Emily blushes. "It's the makeup and the heels."

I shake my head. "And you own this place?"

She purses her lips. "My dad does. I just work here so I can earn extra money."

My face is covered in shame as I mumble, "Oh, God, how old are you?"

Reaching for my hand, she says, "Don't worry. I wouldn't be working in a bar if I wasn't old enough. If it makes you feel better, I'm twenty-two."

My heart skips a beat. I remember when I was twenty-two. Liv and I were like rabbits, fucking each other like there was no tomorrow. It must have ended when she lost the baby. She never looked at me again like how she did. The twinkle in her eye was replaced with bitterness and shame.

Emily pulls me inside. "What do you say you and I... you know."

I can still taste the last spoonful gelato I ate, but all I want to devour is Emily. After locking the door, she pushes me against the table. I allow myself to take it all in, inhaling the sweet jasmine scent from her hair. Emily rubs her breasts against my face while I rip down her panties. I shove myself hard against her, holding her thighs. Her skin feels smooth as silk and smells like honey.

"Oh, Emily, you don't know how you make me feel. It's like being twenty-two again."

She moans and cries a bit each time I release and push. Emily bends down toward the table, and I enter her from behind, rough as she likes it. With a playful spank, she flexes her body up and down. Moments later, we're doing the sixty-nine and I've forgotten how crappy I thought my life was. When it's over, our bodies collapse on the floor.

I trace her nipples and spot the tiny freckles on the bridge of her nose.

She giggles, rises from the floor to grab her sweater, and throws my shirt at me. "You know where to find me."

A big smile plays on my lips. "You bet."

I not only know where to find her, but I've explored more of her waist down then I've done with Liv in the last year. And if this is going to loosen me up a bit before the rage takes over me, then I'm in it for the ride.

* * *

Later over dinner, as Liv stirs her potato leek soup, I hum a tune.

She glances at me and furrows her eyebrows.

I clear my throat. "Can you please pass the olives?"

Liv pushes them close to me. "So, how was your day?"

I almost break into a grin as images of Emily flash through my mind, but instead I give her my poker face. "Same old, same old."

"I'm working till late tomorrow and will need to cover for Janice who is sick."

Spreading butter on my bun, I imagine it's Emily's thighs and continue to hum.

"Are you okay? Did you hear what I said?"

"Sorry. I'll leave the hallway light on." I finish my food.

"Thanks."

From the corner of my eye, I see Liv watching me.

I stride to my office, mulling my next goal. *Have fun no matter what my situation is.*

Day 4

David

Three days before the coma.

Emily and I are lying down on the rooftop of her bar, staring at the sky. I saw her yesterday, but couldn't wait to spend time with her today.

"You're sure your dad's not coming up here?"

"Relax." She lights a joint, takes a puff, and passes it to me. "He's out of town, and the bar doesn't open for four hours."

Don't remember the last time I smoked pot. Gosh, must have been in college with some friends. I take two puffs and lean my head against her shoulder. "So, this is the life, huh?"

"Pretty much." She faces me. "What is it that you do? I don't know anything about you."

"Nothing interesting. I'm a graphic designer."

She rises. "Seriously?"

Seeing the twinkle in her eyes makes me realize this is the approval I seek from Liv.

Pulling her toward me, I nuzzle her neck.

She giggles. "Please tell me more. You're an *artist*."

I like the sound of that. "Well, technically not. I design logos and websites, that sort of thing."

Her eyes glimmer. "You're still an artist."

My heart melts. "Thank you."

"How about you design our website?"

"How can you not own a website? It's the twenty-first century."

Bursting into laughter, she presses her breasts against my chest and stares right into my eyes. "My dad is old school, but I can convince him."

I nibble on her lower lip. "If you say so."

Emily thrusts her tongue inside my mouth. "I hope you're not too pricey."

Pulling her on top of me, I grin. "You can always pay me in kind."

We kiss, but then she pulls away and sits up. "I wanna learn everything about you."

"C'mon." I point to my crotch. "Junior wants you."

She shakes her head, giving me that naughty laugh that lights up her face. I can't stop staring at her. One moment, she looks like an angel, so pure and innocent, yet another side of her is a vixen. If I met Emily back then and we were the same age, would I like her? What if she turned out to be like Liv?

A knot formed in my stomach as I remembered the day Liv stopped talking. We used to chat about anything under the sun, but after three failed pregnancies, all I heard was a slammed door, feet dragging, and the tinkering of knives. Liv never looked at me the same way again. So I locked myself in my office, where I didn't need to see her expression, feel her frustration, or taste her despair. I became a robot going through the motions, and we both allowed work to consume us.

"What do you want to know?"

She takes a puff of the joint then ditches it away. "I dunno. What keeps you awake at night? Do you like chocolate? Why are you so mysterious?"

I sit up and rest my head against the wall. "For starters, I'm boring. The client tells me their concept, and I create the design. I guess it's pretty much the same with my personal life." I pause. Shit! I get it now. Liv finds me boring. Although my life ain't structured like hers, I'm still predictable. Well, guess what, Liv? Today, I learned I'm not going to be predictable anymore.

Emily snaps her fingers. "You were saying something about your personal life."

"Right." I rub my chin. "Why don't we keep it mysterious and learn as we go?"

"Well, aside from you being an incredible kisser, I might have to add I never expected to see you again after the first night. Why'd you return?"

I purse my lips, wanting to enjoy the ride. "How can I resist you?"

She squints and shakes her head. "Next time you come over, I'll take you to my favorite place. That way we can do something else besides fuck."

Laughter explodes from my mouth. "Come here, you naughty girl."

Emily yelps.

Our lips meet, and the next thing I know, we're both naked underneath the blanket.

Liv is asleep when I get home. My mental note for my next goal is *Be prepared for a big change.*

Day 5

David

Two days before the coma.

I push the comforter aside and jolt as I witness Liv standing in front of me. "Goodness, you scared me."

"You said you'd leave the hallway light on." Her stern voice sends a shiver to my spine.

"Sorry, I forgot."

"Where were you? The cat litter is full, and you didn't leave water for Wilma."

I head for the bathroom. She actually trails behind while I piss. "It's late, can we talk about this in the morning?"

"Why do you keep forgetting to do these things?" she harps.

"Damn it!" I flush the toilet. "Just because I work from home doesn't mean I need to do everything."

"We discussed this before." She follows me to the bedroom. "And why is it that I can cook, clean, and do the laundry while working a ten-hour shift?"

"Because you're *Ms. Superwoman* who expects everyone to be like you."

"Where were you today?" She folds her arms.

Plopping into the bed, I cover my body with the blanket. "I met with a client. We discussed his company logo design."

"Your clothes smell like smoke. They look filthy."

I shake my head in disgust. "What am I supposed to do if they smoke? You're fucking unreasonable."

"I don't know what's wrong with you."

"What's wrong with me? How about you ask yourself that question, Liv? How do you think I feel each time you come home and stare at me like I'm some kind of loser?"

She snaps back, "I never said that."

"You don't have to. Your friends think you wear the pants while I just work from home."

"I'm not obliged to explain to them what you do."

"Really? Even the farmer's market vendor knows me as your husband." I fold my arms. This discussion should end now.

"If you have a problem with what people think about you, work on your self esteem."

"You're just so different. Look at how we've become, two angry people. We used to have fun, but now all you do is control me."

"Control you?" She points a finger at me. "How dare you say such a thing? I don't even bother you."

"Yes, you do. You tell me to get the cat litter and keep the light on. Is that all I'm worth to you?"

Liv doesn't say a word as she climbs into bed.

I face the other way. No use arguing with her when all she wants is perfection. Tomorrow, I'm seeing Emily again so she can take me to her favorite place. That should make me feel better.

***

Emily greets me as I arrive at the bar. Her hair is still wet, and she smells like fresh linens. I want to have sex with her, but she takes my hand while we explore the streets of San Francisco. Glad I wore a cap today. If I bump into someone I know, hopefully they won't recognize me.

"Where are you taking me?"

Emily grins, carrying her purse. "You'll see."

Moments later, we arrive at a skate park.

She tugs my arm, but I pull away. "No way!" I glance at a skater swerving on the slopes, smooth and steady while he sways down the hill and releases on the curb. "You're not going to catch me dead on skates. Balancing ain't my strongest suit."

"Silly. I didn't bring you here to skate." She leads the way to the side of the park. Right in front of me is a vibrant abstract mural. Emily reaches inside her purse and removes three cans of spray paint.

"Wow." I admire the bright colors then slant my gaze toward Emily. "You did this?"

Her cheeks turn pink. She sprays on the side outlined. "My mother died when I was four years old. Dad took me here every day." She faces me. "We used to watch people skate for hours without saying a word, but what fascinated me the most..." Tears spill from her cheeks while she continues to work on her art. "A man there painted a mural. I became transfixed in his world."

At a loss for words, I'm hypnotized in her world, seeing the broken child in her and the woman she transformed into. I want to embrace her, but let her maintain what she's doing.

She wipes the tears off her cheeks. "I'm sorry. I hope I'm not boring you."

"No." I rub her back. "I like watching you paint."

A smile spreads on her lips. She hands me a green spray paint. "You try it."

"You sure?" I remove the cap.

"Yeah." She points to a spot. "It's easy. You can do it."

As I spray the concave spots, my body begins to relax and I get lost in the art.

She peers at my work. "I told you you can do it."

I nudge her side. "And you call me the artist. What is this painting?" I study the shapes trying to figure out what it is.

"My creative expression." She shrugs. "I like painting abstracts because life doesn't always have to make sense."

I take a deep breath. She's right. Life doesn't have to make sense. I came to the bar on my birthday looking to get some attention my wife failed to provide me and I found Emily.

She nuzzles her nose against my cheek. We both spray the areas she outlined. "Thank you for coming with me. It meant a lot to me."

I squeeze her hand. Then we stride back to her place. "I enjoyed so much today."

"Maybe you can take me to your favorite place next time."

What is my favorite place? I can't really think. If I asked Liv, it would be something fancy. I had promised to take her to the Eiffel Tower in Paris, but that never happened. Maybe if she were nicer to me , I would. Everything about Emily spelled simplicity. To a four-year-old kid who lost her mother, the skate park was heaven. She reminded me of the way Liv once was.

I stop walking and place my hands on her cheeks. "I don't know where my favorite place is, whether it's at the rooftop of your bar or walking the streets of San Francisco and I know it's only been a few days, but I think I'm falling in love with you, Emily."

Her mouth drops, and her eyes get misty. "Oh, David, I never thought a man like you would want to be with someone like me. I love you too."

We kiss. Deep in my heart, I'm so happy for the first time in a long while and it's all because of Emily. My next goal is to *keep matters simple*.

Day 6

David

One day before the coma.

Shit! Shit! Shit! Pacing around my office like a caged animal doesn't help. I can't sleep. I can't eat. I can't work, and I shaved my chin three times. Call me stupid, but I'm in love. Call it quick, but I know when something is real.

"David," Liv calls out from the bedroom.

I can't face her and told her earlier I have a VIP client and need to focus, but she doesn't get the message.

She pops in. "David, I can't find my facial scrub. Did you see it anywhere?"

Fuck. "Don't you keep it in the bathroom?"

"It's not there." She rolls her eyes.

"I can't concentrate. I'm going to take a walk." I head for the door, but she leans her body against it.

"What's the matter with you these days? You seem... different."

I scowl. "What are you talking about?"

"You're always distracted and can't look at me straight in the eye."

"Please don't act like you care." I fold my arms.

She plants her hands on her hips. "What do you mean I don't care? Who do you think takes care of this house?"

"I've heard that a thousand times. I owe my life to you, Liv."

She glares at me and walks out.

Sighing, I grab my coat and exit our house for the past six years. It didn't feel like *home*. When did Liv change? We used to go on morning runs and weekend hikes, but we kept trying for a child and the pressure built up. Liv had a miscarriage so we worked with fertility doctors, and when that didn't happen, we gave it all up and stopped nurturing each other. I doubt a baby would save our marriage.

Strolling by our favorite roast beef cafe, I believe the memories are now past behind me. I can't stop thinking about Emily and want to leave Liv, yet my gut tells me she'll make it hell for me. She freaks out when I don't throw away the cat litter, much less me wanting a divorce.

But I can't prolong this anymore. I need to leave my wife.

***

Emily opens the front door ajar. "You miss me already?" She plants a peck on my lips.

The truth is, I want to make this sooner. I close my eyes and drown in her kisses. "Can we go to the park?"

"Now?" She glances at her watch. "It's late and freezing."

"I need to talk to you."

Emily steps outside in her Uggs and a hoodie. "My old man's inside, and he can be a grouch." She locks the door and takes my hand before crossing the street.

We enter a cafe and sit by the corner table.

The waiter brings us the menu.

"I'll just have coffee," I say.

"Make it two," she adds.

My hands are clammy, and I'm clueless on how to break it to her.

The waiter brings the coffee.

Emily's eyes light up. "So..." She adds sugar to her cup and stirs her coffee. "What did you want to tell me?"

I take a big gulp of my drink. Fuck! The coffee's hot, and my tongue burns. There's no way I can tell her now. I'm such a coward.

She rubs my leg with her foot, teasing me while she bats her eyelashes.

Taking a deep breath, I gaze into her eyes and can't find the words to say.

With furrowed eyebrows, she shakes her head. "Are you okay?"

"No, no." I lean forward and clutch her hands. "I just wanted to say that yesterday was one of the most memorable days of my life. You struck a chord inside me."

She stares at me.

"You're quite matured for your age, and each day, I learn something from you."

Looking around the cafe, she turns back at me and whispers, "What do you say we go to the bathroom and…"

"What?" I turn to the couple in the opposite end of the cafe as they prepare to leave.

"You know." She winks.

"Here?"

Emily rests her foot on my crotch and straightens her shoulder. "Yes. You never take me to your place so we need to be creative. Follow me in two minutes."

Before I can say anything, she heads to the restroom. I whistle to the waiter for the bill. He comes right up and gives it to me. Then I rest two folded bills on the table and survey the cafe. Nobody seems to be looking at me, so I march to the ladies' bathroom.

Already naked, Emily tugs me inside and locks the door. I lift her to the counter and strip down my pants then push inside her while she clasps her legs around my buttocks. Boy, do I love this woman.

She pulls my head against her breasts, and I inhale lavender and citrus. Eyes shut, I imagine what it would be liked to spend my life with Emily.

Moments later, a knock intrudes our rendezvous. Emily bursts into laughter and jumps down.

"Sh!" I cover her mouth.

"We're closing," a man says.

"Give me a few," Emily responds. She zips her pants.

"How the fuck am I going to get out of here?" I whisper.

Her calm stupor amazes me. "Don't worry about it."

I let her go ahead and count to thirty before I leave. The waiters give us cold stares before we exit the cafe. Like two little kids, we run and giggle as we cross the street.

"I'll see you tomorrow?" she asks.

"Tomorrow." I kiss her on the lips, never wanting to say goodbye.

***

"That was a long walk," Liv says when I enter the house.

Glancing at my watch, the one Liv gave me, I remind myself I should no longer wear it. Too many memories which now felt like spoiled broth. I'd been gone for more than two hours.

"Yup." I hang my jacket on the coat rack. "Need to get my creative juices flowing. Something you won't understand, given you have a real job and I don't."

Without saying a word, Liv retreats to our bedroom while I march to my office and tell myself, *Don't wait till Day Thirty.*

Although I never wrote down my goals, I have it all mapped out. I tuck my notebook inside our old love letters pile—no way would she ever read them again—then stride downstairs to the garage where we store our memories. *Yep, I'm not waiting thirty days.*

Day 7

David

The day of the coma.

Nothing is better than having your accountant and lawyer as a good friend. That's what Mark is to me. He's a busy man, but he always accommodates me. While I'm waiting outside his office, I tap my shoes on the floor. He's running late, and I'm scheduled to meet Emily for lunch. I tried calling her cell phone. No answer so I sent her a text instead. Still no response.

The door swings open, and out comes my buddy, always wearing a suit. Mark exposes a dimple. "Hey, bud. Sorry. Just got off a call with my client. Come in."

"It's cool." I follow him inside and plop into a chair across his desk. Awards and photos are displayed on the wall.

"So, what's so urgent it couldn't wait?"

I sigh, dwelling on the crow perched on a tree outside his window. "Not sure where to begin."

Mark leans back in his chair. "Are you having financial problems? Tax questions?"

"No, nothing like that." I rub my hands on my face. "Did you encounter marital problems with Yvonne?"

He crosses his legs and purses his lips. "Well, yeah, everybody does."

I open my mouth, but can't seem to find a way to spell it out for Mark.

"You're having an affair."

"Right." I heave a sigh. "It's more than that. She's twenty-two and—"

"Twenty-two." He beams, ready to jump from his chair. "Where have you been shopping?"

"Even if I didn't meet Emily, my marriage was doomed a long time ago." My gaze lowers to the carpet as I try to find the subtlest way to explain my situation. "I'm physically present, yet emotionally empty."

"Sorry, bud, I thought you guys were happy."

"We used to be."

"And you're looking for a way out."

I nod.

"As your tax attorney, I can tell you from a practical point of view that you're in the losing end with Liv being the breadwinner."

"I don't care about the money. I can live in a freaking studio if need be."

With one eyebrow raised, he shakes his head. "And do you think Ms. Newby will still like you after that?"

"She's not like that. She's simple."

After he rises from his chair, Mark heads to his putting green and picks up a golf club. He positions a golf ball on the tee and swings the club. Hole in one. "Let me tell you about women, David." He faces me. "The older they get, the bigger the needs. They won't just settle for average."

I scowl, wishing he could offer me a better solution. "Are you saying I should stick it out in my dead-end marriage?"

"Have you tried counseling?"

Rolling my eyes, I get out of my chair. "I don't love Liv. She's not the woman I married. Like you said, she has bigger needs and I'm not the one for her."

"Then get a divorce. There aren't any kids to worry about."

I picture Emily having a sweet boy we can take to the skate park. I'd like to think we can be happy. We can have a future together. Her father will surely turn the bar over to her, and we can live there.

But then my thoughts shift to Liv. "You don't know Liv. She'll make it hell for me."

***

I'm running late when I knock outside Emily's house.

An old scruffy man whom I assume is her father opens the door. "Who the hell are you?"

"I'm looking for Emily." I catch my breath as I zip my jacket.

"She ain't here." He bangs the door shut.

"Fuck!" I try her cell, and it goes directly to voicemail. "Where can she be?"

Right, the skate park.

My hunch proves to be right. Emily is working on the right side of the mural.

She doesn't flinch. "You flake."

"I'm sorry. I tried calling and texting you."

She outlined a circle. "I ran out of battery."

I embrace her from behind, inhaling the scent of paint mixed with cinnamon. "Do you forgive me?"

"It depends."

Wanting to get a closer look, I inch forward, turn her around to face me. Her sunken eyes makes me want to protect her, but I'm not sure if it's Emily the young, vulnerable girl, or Emily the vixen trying to tease me?

"There's still so much I have to learn about you."

"What do you want to know?" My hands grasp her cheeks.

Pursing her lips, Emily says, "Thank God for Google. I found your place."

My heart pounds and I take a step back.

"Relax. Your roommate said you had to meet a client. She's pretty cute, you know."

Eying the skaters with their skateboard muffles the tones of Emily's voice. "My roommate? Right, I don't see much of her."

I hate lying to her, but how do I break it to Emily that I'm married. Where do I begin?

"Neat Victorian home you live in. Maybe next time you can take me there for some afternoon delight."

I force a grin. "Yeah, but hard with a roommate."

"Better than my grouchy dad. And I thought you don't see much of her."

My heart sinks. It's getting more difficult to pretend. "The walls are quite thin."

"Right." She laughs and jumps on me, nuzzling her nose against my neck. Emily always knows how to make me feel better.

We run around the park sharing a laugh like little kids do.

"Emily, whatever happens, I want you to know that I love you. You've been a ray of sunshine for me."

"Stop." She smacks my arm. "You're acting like you're going to die and I won't see you again."

"Nothing like that. Just feel that this is the right moment to tell you how much you mean to me. I'm sure there are guys who'd go crazy over you, but I'm thankful you chose me."

She kisses my nose. "I could say the same about you."

Her soft touch makes me melt. Embracing her tight, I tuck a strand of her hair around her ear and wish this moment would never end. *Tonight, I'll tell Liv.*

***

Before going home that evening, I hop on the Bart train and ride from one end to the other, never getting off till the last stop then going back again to where I started. I need time to think. Nothing makes sense. What's the worst Liv can do to hurt me? She's most likely aware about Emily. Liv's golden rule is for me to never meet clients at home, so I can't lie and claim Emily's a client. Should I tell her Emily is a friend? But since when did I have girlfriends? Considering Mark is my only friend.

I'll tell her I don't know who the fuck Emily is. Yes, that's it.

Feeling beat and tired, I enter the house. Wilma purrs as I hang my coat. The house is dim, but if

I'm not mistaken, I hear faint music. What's that smell? Vanilla or is it cinnamon?

"Honey?"

She hasn't called me that in years.

"Is that you?" Liv calls out.

"Yes."

"I'm in the bedroom."

I creep closer, and the music is louder. Is that a love song?

Opening the door, I step inside and spot Liv on the bed, surrounded by candles.

She pushes the comforter aside and reveals black lingerie. "Come to bed."

All I can think about is Emily.

"Do you want a drink?" She approaches me.

"I'm good."

Massaging my shoulders, she kisses my neck. "You look tired. Let me remove your shirt."

"It's fine."

"I'll fix you a drink." She leaves the bedroom.

I hop out of my clothes and change into my boxers. Not once did she ask me about Emily, but I'm not giving in to her manipulative actions. She's probably using reverse psychology on me. I'm getting a divorce. I don't care what she does. Tonight, I will be a free man.

Liv comes back with two glasses of wine. "Try this."

Taking the glass from her, I tell myself I could surely use a drink. Will help me relax when I tell her. Who cares if I wrote thirty days before I would leave her? I ain't Liv, and I can't follow a schedule. Thirty days is just too much. It needs to be done today.

Taking a huge gulp of the wine, I face Liv. *It's now or never.*

Day 7

Liv

Today is the day our ship will dock, and I need to make a choice if I will go with Aiden and leave Olivia Walters behind. What makes me think I'm so impulsive I could possibly leave my sick husband? Nobody will buy my disappearance and what will happen to David when he regains his memory? I want him to look at my face and remember the love we once shared.

It's too bad. I kinda enjoyed being Red and my rendezvous with Aiden, but the game is over.

All right, I have to be honest with myself. I knew all along David was having an affair. It was spelled all over his face. I smelled it in his clothes. His scent was no longer his. I didn't need to read his thirty-day goal. A woman always knows when a man has been unfaithful.

The truth is, I wanted to feel what David felt when he met that slut Emily. He was going to leave me for that young pathetic bar lady who paints murals at a skate park. How could he do such a thing?

After being with Aiden, I understand David now. The romance causes you to produce that adrenaline rush like you're young, fresh... as if you can do anything. I allowed myself to be his whore purposely, submissive and without wanting to know anything about him to keep the fantasy, only to realize how cheap my husband is to mistake sex with love.

I still can remember the bitch's face the second time she showed up at my place looking for David.

"Hi, I'm sorry to bother you," she said with a twinkle in her eye. "Is David around?"

With my grim face, I folded my arms. "My *husband*'s in a coma."

She had that horrified look as she stammered, "Coma?" She gasped, her shoulders now slump, her face pale like powder. "Wait a minute. Did you just say he's your husband?"

I straightened my shoulders, and my lips formed a fine line. "We've been married for ten years, and who do I have the pleasure of speaking with?"

"Um, uh, I'm so sorry. I'm sorry," was all she could say, and she dashed out of the door.

I never saw her again, but that evening, I passed by the skate park and threw bleach on her mural, making sure to leave it spotless. There was nothing this lady deserved than my vomit.

And so the night when David came home which I assume he spent the day with her, I dressed in my lingerie and put on some music and scented candles to try to lure David into making love to me. I saw the expression on his face, a mixture of confusion and fear. That was when I offered him a drink of wine, so he could loosen up. David, always the coward, took a sip—nope, a gulp. And I waited till the uppers and downers kicked in.

I saw it coming and couldn't deny it. When the person you love collapses right in front of you with eyes flickering like strobe lights at a club, you know damn well you need to call for help. But I didn't. I just stood there, listening to the waves of air emerging from his chest, counting the seconds when he would go. But he stayed, and I was Olivia Walters once again, the nurse who took care of everyone except herself.

So what do I do with Aiden now that he's crazy about me?

One, I can continue to enjoy wild sex with him.

Two, I can use him as my accomplice.

Three, I can manipulate him into having an affair with Emily.

Four, all of the above.

You know what my choice is.

Day 8

David

I'm so tired. What the hell happened? What day is it? My eyes are heavy. Where am I? What the fuck! The TV is blasting, and the weather reporter is talking about the climate. "It's going to be another foggy day in San Francisco."

Where is that slim woman? She told me her name is Liv, my wife. I don't remember her or if we got married.

"Darling." A plump lady massages my arms, but I don't know who the hell she is. "It's just me and you, just like when you were little. Do you remember when we used to make snow cones?"

Is she my mother?

"Where am I?" I pull my arm away.

The lady showers me with kisses, but her voice sounds guarded. I can hear her well. "Don't you worry, David. Liv will be back in a few days. She was stressed and needed a break."

Liv? Did she mean the beautiful lady? Where did she go?

Mom adds, "Hope you don't mind me watching cheesy movies."

Eyeing her, I scratch my head. This is all so confusing.

Mom settles on the armchair beside my bed to my right. "You're such a brave boy."

Why is she talking to me like a little kid? Staring at the TV, I try to patch things together, but I can't make out what's wrong.

When the show ends, Mom rises from her seat and smiles at me. "I need to change your diapers."

Glancing at my plaid pajamas, I jolt. I remember something. I hate plaid. Wait. Did she say diapers?

Not waiting for my response, Mom removes the blanket from my legs. I immediately rest my hands on my lap.

"David, you don't have to be ashamed."

Bolting upright, I try to wiggle my toes, but it takes a lot of effort like a slow motion movie.

Flashing me that tender look, she sends comfort to my fears. She's my mother. I want to reach out to her and ask her what happened, but I'm too scared to know the truth. Am I sick? Am I dying? *Why can't I fucking remember?*

Day 8

Liv

I'm back in my bedroom in San Francisco like it never happened. Did I meet with Aiden again? *No*, but I did send him a message. What's the reason for having a friend when you can't use them? My dear Christopher gave Aiden my card. As with all my lies, I added one more and told Christopher Aiden had been a wonderful chef who made me try different dishes while Christopher spent time with Patrick. I was merely writing a thank you card to show my appreciation for his kind hospitality.

We slept the whole plane ride back from Rome to San Francisco. Rest assured, I needed a peaceful transition from Red to Olivia Walters.

My mother-in-law left as soon as I arrived while I resumed my routine with David. He looks the same except for the pajamas he's wearing. He hates plaid.

Giving me blank stares, David rises from the bed, clinging to my arm. We take baby steps around the room which seems like progress from last time when all he wanted to do was sleep.

His mouth carves into a smile. "Thank you."

An image of Aiden flashes through my mind, sending me jitters down there.

I want to tell him, "In case you're wondering why I haven't killed you yet, it's because I need to finish my thirty-day wisdom project, the one you thought I would never start. Unlike you, I always complete my projects." But I don't.

My mind is still reeling from what he did.

I'm not ready to get rid of you yet. Not till I make your slut suffer. Your coma wasn't enough. She has to feel what I went through when I discovered you were having an affair, but I can't do that alone. I now have an accomplice who has helped me rebuild my self-esteem after you trashed it.

My co-workers and the doctors encouraged me to think positive that David could regain his memory. Miracles do happen, but I like seeing him here helpless and alone. I've turned away visitors because I don't want him to feel loved. I hate him!

The doorbell rings. It's Vienna, the caregiver who watches David. I run downstairs and welcome her inside before I disappear into the night.

***

Aiden strokes my cheek. "I thought I'd never see you again."

We are checked in at the Holiday Inn in San Francisco, and he's glad to live in the same city as I do. A part of me shares the same enthusiasm as Aiden, but another side of me would rather leave that behind. As he gratifies me over and over again, I realize sex is a powerful drug that can entice you to do forbidden things.

"I sent you a card. You know I can't just walk away from my life."

Aiden embraces me from behind. "No more games, Red. For once, let's be honest with each other."

Honesty isn't my best suit. I don't know how many lies I need to maintain what I started, but I need Aiden more than he needs me. "There's a woman I want you to meet," I say slowly.

A grin spreads on his lips. "I didn't know you needed someone else to satisfy you."

"Silly. I don't mean that." I lean forward and reach for my purse to get my iPhone. Googling her, I show him Emily's photo. "That's her."

"She's cute, but not as attractive as you are." He smirks.

"Her name is Emily, and her father owns a sleazy bar along North Beach called Skyline."

"Okay." He yawns. "And what do you need from this Emily?"

"I want you to fuck her."

"What?" Aiden rises from the bed. "What the hell do you think of me? Some guy who fools around?" He shakes his head in disgust. "You and I, this is real."

Wanting to throw up the seafood pasta I ate earlier that evening, I pretend not to hear him. "I want you to fuck her brains out till she falls madly in love with you, and then I want you to dump her like a hot potato and let her feel what it is to lose someone you love." My hand forms a fist.

Aiden stares at me and rushes to my side while I rock myself to and fro and choke between tears. "I'm sorry. She took away the man you loved and you want her to pay, correct?"

I nod.

"Why didn't you tell me in the first place?"

I pretend to sob some more so Aiden can pity me. "I didn't want you to think I was a horrible person."

Aiden holds me tight and rubs my back. "Pain is never easy. My ex-wife cheated on me with my best friend a couple of years ago." The veins on his neck tighten. "Each day I debated whom I should kill, him or her? Or better yet both?"

"Why didn't you?"

"Because it wouldn't bring my life back. The damage was done. There's nothing I can do to fix it."

"But they destroyed your happiness. You could have deprived them of theirs."

Running his fingers through his hair, he says, "I found another way to make me happy. I opened my own restaurant and cook everyday."

"I hate to cook."

We laugh.

"Tell you what. If that's what you want me to do for you, then I'll do it." Aiden pulls me close to him.

"You're serious?" My hand cups his cheek.

"Yeah. Whatever revenge I couldn't do for my ex-wife and best friend, I'll do it for you."

I pick up the wine bottle on my night table and pour two glasses. "Here's a toast to partnership."

"Partners." He clicks my glass.

Later on the way home, I realize plotting revenge is better with an accomplice. *If all else fails, you can always put the blame on your co-conspirator. Lucky for Aiden that he gets to fuck two women. Awful for me that I get to sleep in the same bed with my enemy.*

Day 9

David

I had the most disturbing dream last night, that Liv, the slim woman who is supposed to be my wife, tried to kill me. Replaying the dream, I remember not being able to cry out for help, not being able to move. My heart beats fast, and I'm almost sure I break into a sweat, but darkness envelops me. Where is the other lady who said she's my mom? Am I alone? I can't see. Wait. I hear someone breathing beside me. Desperate to cry, I've never felt so alone.

In my dream, music played in the background, and I could swear I smelled candles. A faint female voice called me to the room. Why was I filled with apprehension? As I entered the room, I spotted Liv underneath the bed covers, only revealing the top of her lingerie. Tilting her head to the side, she giggled and signaled me to come closer. Why was I hesitant to go near her? Liv pushed the comforter down and approached me with a tight embrace. If she was my wife, why did I resist?

Liv picked up the bottle on the nightstand and poured two glasses of wine. My mouth grew dry, and I needed a drink. She handed me my glass, and I took a generous sip. I wasn't sure what happened next. Fuck! Why can't I remember?

The sheets ruffle beside me, and someone rises from the bed and marches to the bathroom. "Liv?"

"Go back to sleep, David."

I can't.

Day 9

Liv

With my binoculars, I perch on the railings across the street from Skyline bar. Not that I don't trust Aiden to perform the job, but playing detective stimulates me.

Aiden has been inside for hours, and if he's lucky, the slut will accept his offer of smoking a joint in his car. Then he can lure her into having sex with him. Aiden is an attractive man. I don't see why Emily wouldn't fall for him.

Moments later, Aiden and Emily step outside. A cold shiver runs through my spine. My plan is working, but why aren't they getting in his car? Aiden helps her put on her jacket as they march down the street.

I trail behind them, pretending to be another pedestrian strolling down the road. Where are they going? Emily seems to be leading the way when they hike two more blocks. To keep up, I take bigger steps. They cross the street, and Aiden takes Emily's hand. She doesn't let go, and both of them are in tune as they walk.

The cool breeze doesn't calm my rage. I want to pounce on her, but I need to maintain my focus. After several more blocks, we reach a park. Emily stops and looks at Aiden. He seems transfixed at her gaze. I want to hit him in the head and tell him it should be *her* crazy about *him*. What is wrong with men? Are they like animals that they can't think with their brains?

Emily tugs him deeper into the woods. The sky is pitch black so I can't see much, but then I realize where we are. *The skate park.*

I'm standing right in front of the mural, the one I poured bleach on, only now the mural is painted with fluorescent and glows in the dark. Not being able to picture exactly what it looks like, I take a step forward and freeze. *What on earth is this?* No way! I weep. It's an abstract face of a man, a face I would have never recognized if I didn't look close enough, a face I can't forget. *David's.*

Straightening my shoulders, I try to keep myself together as Emily rests her hand on his face. *David is mine, not yours.* Emily turns to Aiden, who cups her face with both hands. They stare into each other's eyes. It's a slow-motion scene, like the one you see in the movies when a teenage girl and boy kiss for the very first time. I can almost taste it.

Emily has stolen the moment once again. I will not let her manipulate Aiden. Huffing a sigh, I turn around and break into a sprint for who knows how far or how long. Finally, I stop in the gas station to catch my breath and buy a drink. Fuck! There are two messages from the caregiver but nothing from Aiden.

I try calling Aiden. Voicemail. Fuck! Fuck! Fuck!

***

As soon as I arrive home, Vienna rants at me, "I left you two messages. I have an emergency. My daughter. I have to go."

"Go, go, go!" I wave my hand at her.

"I'll be back next time you need me." She dashes out of the house.

"Don't worry."

Emily loves David, and I hope she doesn't manipulate Aiden. Need to think of plan B. If the accomplice is weak, get rid of the accomplice. Maybe I should get rid of all of them.

Breathe! I need to learn not to do things in haste.

Day 10

David

I'm still perplexed with all that's going on. My wife barely talks to me, and she never touches me.

Something happened to me, but how?

Although Liv doesn't communicate with me, I can feel the tone of her anger when she opens the shutters of the blinds in the morning. As the sun spills inside our bedroom, I know she's always on the phone texting and I hear her fingers tinkering when my eyes are closed.

We go through the routine—baths, change of diapers, walks, and crossword puzzles—but I notice she looks sad.

She spends a lot of time in the bathroom. I seem to hear things more clearly now, and I recognize patterns. The sprinkling of the shower and the flushing of the toilet provide comfort to the stillness of the night. Liv never watches TV, and the remote is always on her side while she sleeps. I wish she would leave it on for me so I'm not consumed by my thoughts. We talk about simple things, but she seems in a hurry to leave.

I wish she could stay because my thoughts invoke every emotion inside me lately. I've tasted fear, loneliness, despair, and hopelessness, and all I know Liv is hiding something.

The clinking of her sandals intrudes my thoughts. A whiff of perfume enters my lungs, and I imagine her dressed in a black dress and lust washes upon me. I'm about to compliment her on how beautiful she is, but that moment is stolen from the sound of the doorbell.

My heart beats profusely as Liv rushes down the stairs. Where is she going again? Why does she keep leaving me? Oh my God! Is Liv going out on a date?

I hear a return of footsteps and my emotions subside. Instead of Liv returning, I smell another scent. It overrides the sweet jasmine Liv had earlier. Now the whole room is filled with a scent of tea rose.

"*Buenas noches, Señor* Walters."

Footsteps march to the bathroom. Moments later, she returns and puts a towel on top of my chest as she mumbles more in Spanish. What is she doing with my shaver? I want Liv to shave me. God forbid, I failed Spanish in high school and take no interest in the language.

She leans her body above me, and her chest touches my nose. A glimpse of my morning ritual shave enters my mind. I remember now. Yes, I used to shave every morning, but never in these pajamas.

"Vienna," she mutters. "Vienna shave you, okay?"

"Okay." Great! That memory is now destroyed by the foul odor of her perfume.

I allow my eyes to follow where the shaver is going, but then she stops. A sting rubs my chin.

"Sorry, sorry." She dabs my chin.

Great, Vienna cut me. I want to yell at her to put some shaving cream on me, but she won't understand me. I pray, hoping she hasn't injured me yet. The motor sound tries to lull me to sleep, but my adrenaline is so strong and I want to get out of bed.

Moments later, the sound stops and I believe I dozed off. I know Vienna is in the bathroom because I can hear the faucet running. The scent of her perfume stays with me.

"Achoo."

Did I just sneeze? Yes, I heard it right. Fuck, I can't be stuck here. I'm going to spend the next hour trying to walk without help. Mind over matter and will power and all that.

Vienna talks to me. "Clean now, *Señor* Walters."

I hear a splashing sound then like she's squeezing water out of a face towel. Oh God, Vienna is going to give me a sponge bath. Liv should be home with me.

Something's not right here. My wife is hiding something.

Day 10

Liv

After the tenth call, Aiden finally picks up.

"Please tell me you didn't sleep with her on the first night." I whisper, pacing around my kitchen like a hamster on a treadmill.

"I thought you wanted me to fuck her."

I never thought Aiden would take me seriously. "Where is she?"

"Relax. I'm home."

"But you did fuck her?"

"Is that a rhetorical question?" he chides.

"Damn it, Aiden."

"Of course I did. Do you want to know how many times she came?"

I don't say a word. Wow!

"It's all part of the plan, Red."

I sigh, my stomach queasy again. "What did she tell you?"

"For starters, we had drinks at her bar. Then she told me she needed some air. That's when she took me to the skate park. You were there."

"I noticed how you looked at her, Aiden."

"I'm a good actor. What can I say?"

A frown crosses my lips. "Did she buy it?"

"Emily said it was a relief to talk to a stranger. She's been mourning over David these past months and she turned her grief into something beautiful."

"And?" I grit my teeth, knowing how this woman can used her charm to make Aiden fall for her.

"When people ask her who the man is, she tells them it's a man she often dreams about, a man who haunts her in her sleep. It's part true, she says. She sees him in her dreams, and she believes they have unfinished business together."

"Did she tell you he's married?"

"Yes, but she claimed she wasn't aware about it."

"Bullshit!" I kick the wall.

"So where is your husband now, Red?"

I pretend I don't hear him. "How did the kiss come about?"

"It was when she laid her hand on the mural of David. I could feel her emotion, her vulnerability, and that's when I knew the time was right. I took advantage of her emotions."

"You did an amazing job." I set my glass on the sink.

"She's quite profound, if you ask me. Never expected that from a twenty-two-year-old."

I almost choked. Twenty-two? Gosh, David, what were you thinking? "The idea is for you to manipulate her. Not the other way around."

"Of course. Don't underestimate me, Red. I know what I'm doing, and hopefully after this is over, we can be together."

Together? How can he be so serious about this? Aiden is in a make-believe world thinking there is an *us*. I might as well play along.

"Are you seeing her again?"

"Yup, taking her out on a real date tonight."

"Where? I want to see you guys for myself."

"All right. We're having dinner at Cactus along Market Street."

"That's too noisy."

"Trust me, Red. It will work out."

I shut the iPhone and throw it inside my purse. *My plan seems to be working. Pretty soon Emily and Aiden will be an item, and she'll forget about David.*

***

Later that evening, the waiter escorts me to the left corner table inside the Cactus Restaurant and Bar. He pulls out my chair then hands me the menu.

My eyes sweep the crowd. Only a few tables are still empty. Glancing at the dinner selections, I zero in on the steaks. I'm craving a juicy one. I snap my fingers at the waiter.

With eager smiles, he approaches. "Would you like to order wine and appetizers while you're waiting?"

Lips pursed, I address him, "I'm not waiting for anyone. I would like a ribeye, medium rare—and red wine. That's all." I give him a faint smile, one that should admonish his presumptions of me having a date.

Instead, he expresses a wider smile. "Very well, madam. I will ensure that you get the juiciest steak."

"Thank you."

There's no sign of Aiden and Emily. I check my iPhone. No messages. Minutes pass by quickly, and they're still not there.

"Waiter."

"Your steak is coming out."

He's being presumptuous again. "That's not why I'm calling you."

"I'm very sorry, madam." He blushes.

"Is this the only Cactus restaurant in San Francisco?"

"The one and only, madam. Here comes your steak." He points to another waiter who brings the plate.

I nod, but my appetite disappears.

My eyes dart toward the clock before I slice the steak and take a bite. The meat melts in my mouth as desired, and I imagine Aiden's supple lips. I continue to chew, slice and chew again, going through the motions as the clock ticks. Still no Aiden and Emily.

Once I'm done with my meal, I take a long gulp of the wine and call Aiden. Directly to voicemail. After ten voicemails and fourteen texts, my mouth grows arid. I bite hard, and the salt and charred aftertaste of the steak is now substituted by my own flesh.

After paying my bill, I flee into the busy streets of San Francisco. Where could they be? Despite my heels, I run across the street and head for the skate park, only to find out they aren't there.

A man wearing a hooded sweater approaches me. "Do you have a light?"

Startled, I take a step back. "I'm sorry. I don't smoke."

He inches so close to me I'm forced to get a good view of his face—auburn hair, droopy eyes, and thick dark circles. His fingernails are filthy, and he could use a shower. "Why are you here?"

"I'm sorry. I must have gotten lost. I'll head back now." I take larger steps.

"You shouldn't come here wearing that."

"He's right." Another man appears from behind him.

"I'm sorry. I got lost. I need to go home now."

The other man looks like his brother, only much taller than him. Narrowing his gaze towards my legs, he adds, "What's the matter? Are you scared of us?"

I need to think quickly. These men won't harm me if I know how to play the game. Taking a deep breath, I smile. "Oh, not at all. I'm glad I'm not alone. Do you think you guys can walk me back to the main road?"

They exchange glances and shrug.

"Sure," the first man says.

A hand rests on my chest. "Thank you. I can also get you a lighter at the store and a drink too. It's on me."

They lighten up and lead me back to the main road. "You're safe now," the taller man says.

I dig into my purse, pull out a twenty, and hand it to him. "Here."

He takes it. "Thanks."

I nod then cross the street, staying with a crowd for some time to calm my nerves before heading home. Phew! I'm not risking myself again. If Aiden wants to play this game, he better do it on my terms.

Once I reach home, I remind myself *never to trust anyone.*

Day 11

David

Liv leaves me again under the care of Vienna. She seems very distracted, always on the phone or pacing around the room. I can't hear what Liv says, but the sound of her clicking heels tells me she's seeing someone special.

Vienna watches Spanish *telenovelas,* and she sheds a tear once or twice. I enjoy listening to them too despite not understanding a thing. It's better than thinking. I need to use my body more.

Last night, I had a recurring dream of Liv trying to kill me. Did she put something inside my wine?

Vienna rises from her chair and passes by my bed to go to the bathroom. Her hips hit my foot. Without hesitation, I rise from my bed, slowly exit the bedroom, and head down the stairs.

I can do it! I don't need anybody's help. Exhaustion creeps under my skin, but I continue to push forward. An image of my mother flashes through my mind. She used to say, "David, never give up."

Yes, I will not give up.

Day 11

Liv

Christopher rests on the living room couch as I stir my tea. There are nineteen days before I go back to work and decide what I will do with David and my life. This needs to be planned thoroughly.

"The last time I saw you was on the cruise," he muses.

"I'm sure Patrick keeps you preoccupied."

"Sure." He waves his hand in the air. "I'm sorry if I've been neglecting you."

"I've been busy as well." I cross my legs, wishing I could tell him everything and wondering how he would react if I did.

"How's David? Any updates?"

"He's walking and talking, but he hasn't regained his memories."

He frowns. "Don't you hate that? How can you move on with your life? How do you even manage to live?"

Tears prickle my eyes. Perhaps I shouldn't have drugged him, but I remind myself what he did to me.

"I'm sorry. I didn't mean to upset you."

"I need to tell you something." I can't keep my secret anymore.

"What is it?" He straightens his shoulder.

Rising from my seat, I pace around the living room. How do I break it to him? "Before David slipped into a coma, I discovered he was having an affair."

Christopher covers his mouth. "No."

"Yes." There, I finally spit it out.

"David? David crazy-in-love David?"

"Yes. My intuition told me that he was going to break the news of leaving me." I wipe the tears from my face. "We had a fight, and he wouldn't stop screaming. I told him to calm down, but he pushed me into the corner. If only you saw the rage in his eyes…"

"My goodness. I never anticipated David to act that way."

"Me neither. I slapped him and… just when he was about to hit me, he paused and then collapsed on the floor. His eyes still open." I cover my face and sit down on the couch. "For a moment, I didn't do anything. I hated him with all my heart, and I actually wished he would die. B-but then I came to my senses and called 911. It's my fault,

Christopher. My emotions stole the better part of me, and because of that, David is this way."

"No, sweetie." He embraces me from behind. "You can't do this to yourself. You're human, and it's not your fault. You're a saint to take care of him after what he did to you. You heard what the doctors said. He mixed uppers and downers with his drinks. It wasn't your fault."

I sob louder, facing him. "W-what would you have done if... if Patrick did that to you?"

"Trust me, lady, I would have killed the motherfucker!" He giggles before turning more serious. "You need to get over this."

"That's why I went on a cruise. So I could forget."

Christopher continues to hold me tight. "This isn't your fault, okay? You're a strong woman, and you need to be kind to yourself."

I nod.

"If we need to go on another cruise to help you heal, let's do it."

We both laugh, and a heavy load releases from my chest. At least I told Christopher half the truth.

"Who was the woman he had an affair with?" he asks gently.

"Some twenty-two-year-old slut whose daddy owns a bar."

"Yikes. Did you meet her?"

"She came here looking for him the day before and the day after he had a coma."

"The nerve of her," he growls.

"Exactly. I wanted to pull her eyeballs out."

"Perhaps she didn't know?" He raises his eyebrows.

I thought of the young waiter at the Cactus restaurant who assumed I had a date. Was Emily presumptuous that David was single? "She's partly to blame for David's decision to leave me. If David didn't slip into a coma, he would have fled with her and what does that leave me?"

Christopher hands me the tea from the coffee table. "I know it's easier said than done, but you'll get over this." He pauses. "And someday, when David is well, you'll rebuild what you lost."

"*If* he gets well." A faint smile spreads on my lips.

"That's what hope is about."

Hope. Where was hope when my parents left me in a dumpster? An elderly couple found me barely breathing and malnourished two days later. They were too old to raise me so they gave me to their crack head neighbors. I moved from foster home to foster home. The only time I had hope was when I met David. Just when I thought for once he could take care of me, it became the other way around. Eventually, his passive complacent nature turned me off. It was up to me where my future lied, so I became a nurse, thinking I could heal and fix a broken wound, yet nobody taught me how to mend a broken heart.

I'm still looking for you, hope. Are you out there somewhere?

Christopher squeezes my hand.

I shake my head. "What can I say? My life is so complicated."

"You're not alone, dearie." He winks.

As Christopher bids me goodbye, I check my phone to see if there's any calls from Aiden. Surprisingly, there's one voicemail from him.

"Sorry, Red, there was a change of plans. I'm here at the Holiday Inn, room three two six. Meet me here when you can."

The caregiver should be coming soon, but not soon enough.

***

I sit on the bed at the Holiday Inn hotel room with my arms folded.

"Why are you so cold?" Aiden asks with his chest exposed.

"You know why."

"I said I was sorry. My phone died, and I couldn't charge it till later."

"You made me wait there like a fool."

Aiden shoved the comforter aside. "Emily suggested she and I go to this new club *Valve*. She was in the mood to go dancing so we had appetizers instead, and after rocking the night, I had her for dessert here in this room."

"You disgust me, you know." I scowl.

"Hey, you're the one who told me to fuck her brains out and make her fall for me. That's exactly what I'm doing."

I flash him a dark look, one I mastered giving to David when I didn't approve of what he was doing.

"Is that all you're going to give me? How about, "Congratulations, Aiden, for a job well done'? I am working for free."

"Do you want me to pay you?" I toss the wine glass on the floor. It shatters into pieces. "Is that what this is about?"

He holds up his hands. "I've never seen you angry. Maybe this isn't a good idea."

Squeezing my hands, I can't get carried away. "I'm sorry. I just got worried when I didn't hear from you."

He reaches for my hand then pulls me toward the bed. "You have to trust me in this. I know she's starting to fall for me." Opening the drawer of the nightstand, Aiden pulls out a USB and gives it to me. "Proof I fucked her brains out."

I expose a lopsided grin.

"I'm seeing her again tomorrow."

"Really? Where?"

"We haven't decided that yet."

My shoulders slump.

"You gotta be flexible, Red. You don't always have to keep an eye on me." He nuzzles my neck with his nose. "After this is done, we can take a cruise again and relive how we first met."

My mind spins. Why does Aiden get to decide what I should do? This isn't right. I can't lose control.

"But tell me something, Red, why didn't you tell me your husband was in a coma?"

Day 12

Liv

Aiden's interrogation yesterday pushed me to my limits. I need to know how to set boundaries with him. David snores the night away, but that doesn't stop me from watching the video of Aiden and Emily from my iPad. The video takes a good shot of Emily on top of Aiden while she moans.

David can sleep even if there's an earthquake. Even if he doesn't hear the video, all I want to do is torture him.

"So you think she loves you?" I glare at him. "I told you she's a slut. She fucked this random guy she met on the first day."

David doesn't flinch.

"The trouble with you, David, is that you think with your dick. You don't have the balls. You never did."

He just lies there like a fallen leaf on the ground.

"Even in your weakest moment, you can't defend yourself. Mind you, she brought this man to the skate park as well. I need to give her credit for painting such a beautiful mural of you. Sad to say, the minute she met Aiden, she forgot about you. I guess that's what Emily and you share in common. You're both sluts."

Rising from the bed, I exit the bedroom and head downstairs to finish watching the video and have some chocolate ice cream.

Sprawled out on the couch, I fast forward past the sex scene and increase the volume.

"So, that guy in your mural, who is he?" Aiden strokes her shoulder.

"An old friend."

"Just a friend?"

Her chest rises with each breath she takes.

"We don't need to talk about it," Aiden says.

Boy, he is good.

Biting her lip, she mutters, "I met him at the bar, and we hit it off really well. He's simple and had no qualms. I like that about him." She smiles then wells up. "I'm not really good with relationships, and I thought he and I had that connection..."

"So what happened?"

"Long story. I found out he was married." She shakes her head. "The sad part is that I went to his house looking for him, and his wife told me he was in a coma."

Aiden embraces her. "I'm so sorry. I'm sorry." He cups her face with both his hands and kisses her.

She weeps like a little girl. "I didn't know he was married. He said he wanted to tell me something one time." Emily bites her lip before nodding. "That's it. It was the night before he slipped into a coma."

"Do you think he was going to leave his wife?"

"I don't know. And the day after, someone went to the skate park and bleached the mural I was working on."

"That's awful." Aiden wipes her tears.

"Yeah, and every day I went back to the park, hoping to paint what I had lost, but David's face kept flashing upon me. I couldn't sleep. I hardly ate. My dad was so worried about me. He threatened to send me to a shrink if I didn't get my act together. "

"Wow."

"Then I had an epiphany." A smile spreads on her lips. "Whatever love I had for David, I would pour it out on my mural. I went to the park during sunrise and left at sunset. I became relentless. I may not be with David, but he'll always be a part of me."

My nails dig into my palms. I can't listen any more, yet I can't bring myself to turn it off.

"This David is a lucky guy," Aiden says.

"Not so lucky with his current condition."

"Right. I'm sorry."

Emily caresses his cheek. "Thank you for listening to me. I'm glad I met you."

"And I could never be more thankful." He wraps his arm around her, obviously getting ready for a second go around.

I roll my eyes. Aiden seems to be enjoying too much.

The front door swings open then shuts. Glancing at my watch, I furrow my eyebrows. It's too early for Vienna. After rising from my seat, I peep outside the window, but nobody is there. I march up the stairs back to the bedroom and mumble, "Vienna, is that you?"

My body freezes.

The bed is empty. There is no sign of David.

"David?" I rush to his side of the bed, but he hasn't fallen onto the floor.

Fuck!

"David?" I dash to our walk-in closet then to the bathroom. "This isn't funny."

I flee back downstairs to our living room, kitchen, and outside.

No sign of David anywhere.

Crossing the street, I ring our next door neighbor's doorbell.

Jake pops out. "Liv, can I help you?"

"I'm sorry to wake you up in the middle of the night, but have you seen David?"

He squints. "David?"

I sigh. "Yes, my husband has just disappeared."

His mouth forms a big "O."

***

After searching for David around the block, I have no choice but to call the cops.

Soon, Officer Cane and I are seated at the living room. She tucks a strand of her auburn hair around her ear. "Do you think he went to visit a friend?"

I shake my head. "David's still suffering from memory loss." I relay about his coma.

Her mouth forms a thin line as she jots down notes. "And where were you when this happened?"

"Right here in my dining room."

Slanting her gaze toward me, she nods. "What was he last wearing?"

"Plaid blue pajamas."

"My partner is still checking with the neighbors. Do you mind if I look around the house?"

"Feel free."

I'm still in shock. I can't believe David would disappear like that. Where would he go? How far can he walk without assistance? Oh God! And if he was found, would he remember what happened? Is that why he left?

Officer de la Torre, a tall, pale man with freckles, pops inside the house. "I've checked with the neighbors and the kids playing down the block. Nobody seems to have seen David."

My sob turns into wails. Blood rises to my head, and I cover my face. I've never anticipated this day would come. David remembers everything and has gone to see Emily. It's all my fault. I've been so distracted lately with Emily and Aiden that I failed to focus on David.

My head spins, and I'm about to faint. This can't be happening. *I can't lose David.*

Day 12

David

My heart jolts me from my sleep. All of a sudden, a surge of pain spikes through both my legs. It's so painful it's killing me, but you don't know how happy I am to feel pain. Adrenaline washes upon me. Liv doesn't know I heard everything she said. She met that man, Aiden, at the cruise while she left me here. Liv tried to kill me, and now she's using Aiden to keep Emily away from me. Emily, my dear Emily. I remember everything now.

While recovering from my coma, I've learned to rely on my other senses. When your judgment fails you, you don't realize how much strain you put on your intuition, but it also teaches you to be vigilant and aware of your surroundings. I'm so sensitive to my thoughts, and I'm glad I trusted my instinct. Now I know why anxiety haunted me that night. It was real. Yes, Liv tried to kill me.

Tears fill my eyes. My dear Emily. I have to save her. I peek around, and I don't see Liv. Now is my chance. I rise from my bed, exit the room and head downstairs. Opening the door, I tell myself to never look back.

***

Today is a new day. I feel like the fog has disappeared. I'm alive, and a ray of sunshine has granted me my first wish.

I was so ready to tell Liv I would be leaving her. Why did I drink the wine she gave me? If only I used my head. Too late to think about that now. Thank God for that hobo who gave me his jacket. Boy, does it stink. I need to get to Emily quick.

Each step makes me pant until I finally reach Emily's house and ring the doorbell. I hope her dad isn't home.

The door opens, and Emily screams.

I cover her mouth. "Sh! Let me in. I can explain everything," I gasp.

Emily catches her breath. "Your wife."

"Please let me in, and if anybody comes looking for me, don't answer the door."

She nods and pulls me inside. We go upstairs to the roof deck. I remove the filthy jacket.

Emily continues to stare at me like I'm some kind of ghost.

"Liv thought she could outsmart me. I'll make sure Liv pays for what she's done."

There's no turning back now. Before I left, I stole her phone and I went through some of her emails between her and her lover Aiden.

Oh my gosh. What did I get myself into?

She calls Emily a slut, but Liv is worse than a Goddamn whore. The lesson for Liv is to not be so presumptuous.

I realize now I married a psychopath and how Liv turned me into an accessory to serve her ego. "She's not capable of love. She has no remorse, Emily, and anything that doesn't benefit her, she will destroy."

Emily burst into tears and wraps her arms around me. "I never thought I would see you again. Look at you, as good as new."

Tears trickle down my cheeks. Gazing into Emily's eyes reminds me of the day we first met. "There's a reason for everything, Emily, and if Liv thinks she can win, she will have to play by my rules to fight."

"Let's call the cops."

"No cops. For now, I want the cops to think she's responsible for my disappearance. Let her suffer, Emily."

"But they'll come looking for you." Beads of moisture appear in her forehead.

"I have a plan. You can't stop seeing Aiden."

She covers her face in disgust. "It didn't mean a thing. I needed someone to help me forget."

"I understand." I kiss her. "Which is why I want you to continue seeing him like nothing happened. Please trust me. I failed you once, and I will not fail you again."

***

Five hours have passed since I left home and with the help of Emily, I've checked into a dingy motel where nobody recognizes me. There's enough food, water, snacks, clothes Emily stole from her father, and her old laptop to keep me going till I fulfill my plan. Emily and I have two disposable cell phones where we'll communicate once a day when I call her. For now, I'll think and plan. My leg hurts, but, man, for a coma victim, I feel good. I'm reborn.

Liv. Her phone. After grabbing it, I head to the bathroom and record a video.

"Hi, Liv, or shall I say Red? Guess where I am? I'm on the fucking toilet taking a *shit*. That's right. No more diapers. I can finally take a crap on my own. I can even record this video from your phone." I cackle. "You thought you could outsmart me? Well, guess what? How about we play a game of hide and seek? Whoever finds the other first gets to kill that person." I point to the camera. "Remember that I'm always watching you."

I replay what I recorded then send it to her email from her email account. That serves her right. Bitch! *She's going to burn in hell for what she did to me.*

Day 13

Liv

"I told you he stole my phone, Aiden." I transfer the cordless on my right ear, hoping to get a better reception. "I'm getting a new one."

"How many times do you have to lie to me, Olivia Walters?"

I bite my lip.

"That's right. I had to hear your real name on the news today," Aiden snaps.

"I'm sorry, okay? I don't need this pressure now."

"I've been transparent with you all this time. What is end game for you?"

The word echoes in my ears as I turn on my laptop. Arguing with Aiden isn't going to take me closer to my goal of finding my husband.

"I'm not benefiting from this, Olivia."

"You're screwing two women. What more do you want?" My voice rises, almost shrill.

"You need to pay me for my services."

"Is that what's this about? I can pay you. Tell me your fees."

"Half a million dollars."

I almost laugh. "I don't have that kind of money."

He exhales. "Oh, but you will when you kill your husband." His voice is more tender now. "Wasn't that your intention?"

Silence crosses between us. What is my end game? I need to think fast.

"You think I don't read between the lines. I'm sure you had him raise his insurance policy before he the coma. Don't worry. I only need ten percent as a down payment. Fifty thousand in my bank tomorrow."

I kick the chair. "Are you blackmailing me?"

"Only if you want me to." He shuts the phone.

I throw the cordless on the bed. Fuck! I'm in a deeper mess than when I started and never anticipated Aiden to turn this way. But then I recall his renal failure and an idea pops in my mind.

My email beeps. Two emails, actually, one from Aiden with his bank account details and another one from myself.

I open it and gasp. *David.*

"Hi, Liv, or shall I say Red? Guess where I am? I'm on the fucking toilet taking a shit. That's right. No more damn diapers. I can finally take a crap on my own. I can even record this video from your phone." He laughs. "You thought you could outsmart me? Well, guess what? How about we play a game of hide and seek? Whoever finds the other first gets to kill that person." He points at the camera. "Remember that I'm always watching you."

I shut my laptop and pace around the room. Should I go to the police? Will they believe me?

What can I learn from all of this? Two wrongs don't make a right. I grin, realizing I have to do what any normal wife would do when her husband goes missing. *Grieve. With an audience. Win their sympathy, and prove that I, Olivia Walters, am a very, very good wife.*

Day 13

David

A stack of index cards is sprawled on my bed. If I have to keep my ducks in a row, I'll need to write down Liv's characteristics and how her mind works. I pick up one and write her traits and history, jotting down notes and sticking them on the wall chronologically.

1. Detail-oriented, planner, superwoman, neat, organized, ambitious, control freak.

2. Left in a dumpster when she was a baby while real parents were crack heads.

3. Moved from one foster home to another. Adoptive parents died in a fire when she was seventeen.

4. Gets what she wants when she wants and how she wants it.

5. Hates competition and will do anything to win.

6. Has to be number one and if she's not, then the center of attention.

I try to analyze what type of game Liv is playing. Why didn't she just call me point blank when she had a chance?

There's a psychological war between us. She always felt superior to me, and because of that, Liv never anticipated I would leave her. Again, Liv assumed she had me wrapped around her finger.

That's it!

I scribble down in bold letters "control." Liv is afraid of losing control. She made me seem like I was a loser. All Liv ever wanted was for me to suffer so she can show to the world what a wonderful caretaker she is. While I was recovering from my coma, she wanted to destroy Emily but needed an accomplice to do it.

The cops are watching her, and I know she's furious with the video message I sent her. To get to me, she'll have to go through Emily. *I gotta think fast.*

I lie down on the bed. My mind is sharper in this position when I can pretend I can't use my muscles. Listening to every breath I take, I watch the rise and fall of my chest, and finally I know how this will all play out.

My dear Olivia Walters, you're going to tell everyone what a bastard of a husband I am.

Shaking my head in disgust, I realized that I, too, need an accomplice.

Day 14

Liv

After printing thousands of flyers of David, I post them on every block. For the first time in my life, I look like a mess. My hair is disheveled, and my clothes don't match. My eyeliner is smeared all over my face so I appear to be crying all night. I welcome the stares of the neighbors as I march along.

Later that afternoon, I return home and shut the door. The cops assigned a detective for the missing case, and I hope they're not suspicious about me. Detective Reed should be arriving any minute now.

The doorbell rings, and I open the door, welcoming the petite, blond detective inside my home. She eyes the stack of flyers scattered around the floor then slants her gaze on the cat poop beside it. Wilma curls behind my legs and purrs. This would never have happened, but I need to show I'm grieving.

"I'm sorry." I pick up the flyers and wipe the poop. "Can I get you anything?"

"No thank you."

She surveys the rest of the house while I escort her to sit down on the couch.

"So, Mrs. Walters, any word so far concerning your husband's whereabouts?"

I shake my head.

"I understand he was a graphic designer working from home, correct?"

"Is," I hiss.

"Right." She nods, not once losing composure or revealing any sense of emotion. "Do you think we would be able to look at his computer?"

We climb the stairs to David's office. Darkness greets us as we enter. Turning on the switch, Detective Reed beams when she spots three monitors and two laptops on top of an L-shaped desk. Strobe lights hang on the wall with a background of Led lights. "Wow!"

"As you can see, he doesn't only work with one computer."

"You must be so proud of him."

All I can give her is a faint smile. An epiphany comes to my thoughts. That's it. I need to tell David I'm proud of him. I need to show him my humility, that I was wrong.

"Do you think I can send my technicians here to go over his computers?"

"Sure. If they can help us find him, that would be great."

"I know this may sound silly, but where would your husband possibly go?"

I liked how she insinuated *your husband* to make it sound so personal, but I wasn't going to tell her about the video David just sent me. If someone has to find David, it will be me. *I* was his *prize*. There's a possibility I can make David love me again, but first I need to get rid of Aiden and Emily.

My cell phone rings, and I welcome the interruption. "I'm sorry." I motion to the detective. "I need to take this call."

Heaving a sigh, I excuse myself and stride downstairs to the kitchen.

"I still haven't received my money," Aiden harps once I answer.

"Look, Aiden, I don't think it's easy for me to do that. Everybody is watching me," I mumble.

"How about I make it easier for you? Let me pick you up and let's drive to the bank together."

"I'm supposed to be grieving, you fuck." I cover my mouth.

"Okay, then you can withdraw the money from different banks. Tomorrow, noon. Be ready." He hangs up.

I clench my fists together.

The detective appears. "He has an amazing work station. With an office like that, you never need to leave home."

"David's very good at his work."

My mind is ticking, and I need to get away from Aiden. What does a grieving wife do? She can get away, right? But first I need to make it clear to David I love him.

After the detective leaves, I dash to my room and ransack my desk in search of the business card I almost threw away. *Bingo! David, you're going to get the surprise of your life.*

Day 14

David

"Honey, when am I ever going to see you?" Emily whines on the phone.

I lean my head against the pillow of the motel room. "I need you to be patient until I figure out how this is going to unfold."

"I'm scared. What if Liv does something to me?"

"As long as you go with the flow with Aiden, everything should be fine." I remove a beer from the fridge and take a sip. Scattered on the table are donuts, potato chips, sour candy, and now my beer. My taste buds are acting out, and I need to give in to my cravings. "Have you been seeing him?"

"I did yesterday, but only for a bit. I told him I needed to help my dad with the inventory of the bar." She sounds exasperated. "But he kept insisting I see him after, and today I let his call go to voicemail."

"You can't do that. It'll be so obvious."

"Please don't tell me what I can and cannot do."

I like the firmness of her voice. Shows me she's an adult responsible for her own actions. Guilt eats me up on the inside, and I hate having to drag her further into this mess. "You're right. I'm sorry."

"I'm going to tell Aiden I heard you're missing and I don't feel comfortable seeing him anymore since I haven't grieved the loss of our relationship yet. I don't have feelings for him. I just needed someone to comfort me while you were gone, David."

Although this would piss Liv off, Emily *is* better off being shielded from these two psychopaths. "When are you going to tell him?"

"I'm not talking to him anymore. I'll just text him."

That could aggravate him. "Listen, Emily, is there somewhere safe where you can stay for the moment?"

"Yes. With you."

Emily is willing to risk everything for me, despite the uncertainty of my situation and how much pain I've caused her. "I never apologized for not telling you I was married."

"You did more. All those months while you were in a coma, I still felt your presence surround me. It's like you never left."

I need to keep Emily safe. I care about her so much and can't hurt her anymore. "Let me call you back. I'll figure something out. Hang in there."

She heaves a sigh. "I love you, David."

Gripping the phone, I say, "I've never stopped loving you."

Using the same disposable phone, I call Mark. I know I can trust him.

He picks up after two rings.

"It's me."

"Jenny, please tell my next client I'm running late," he says to his assistant. "Where the fuck are you?" he asks in a hushed tone.

"Never mind where. I'm safe and okay. I need your help."

"Everybody's looking for you. Your face is in every goddamn convenient store and all over the news."

"I know, I know." I plop a potato chips inside my mouth.

"What the hell do you think you're doing?"

I tell him about what happened, what Liv did to me and that my memory has returned.

There's a long pause. Then all I hear is, "Fuck."

"I can't believe I didn't figure that out. I visited you several times, but she always seemed protective over you. Never wanted the company."

"She's out to get me, but I'm going to get her first." My hands curl into a fist.

"What are you planning to do?"

Averting my gaze outside the window, I take a deep breath and exhale. "I need to fake my death."

"What?" he yells. "Are you fucking crazy?"

"It's the only way she'll leave me and Emily alone."

"The twenty-two-year-old. Are you having a mid-life crisis?"

"Nothing like that. If you meet Emily, you'll see how much substance there is to her."

"Why do you have to fake your own death?"

"Liv doesn't want to lose, and she's going to show to the whole world what a good wife she is. She's going to win everyone's sympathy, but she'll be ruined after everyone thinks she killed me."

He sighs. "And how are you going to pull this off without a body?"

"That's where creativity lies, my friend, and where I'll need you."

Papers rustle. I know he's contemplating whether or not to help me.

"I'm not going to keep you. Sleep on it and I'll call you the same time tomorrow." I hang up.

Perched on the couch, I turn on the TV to watch the six o' clock news. My face flashes on the headlines. What my poor mother must be going through.

The newscaster announces, "Tonight at ten an exclusive interview between Olivia Walters and Chuck Small. Everything you didn't know about David Walters and a marriage gone sour."

WTF! Chuck Small? "You actually had the courage to call Chuck Small. He originally wanted to interview foster kids like you. Didn't you find him annoying, Liv? I knew you would have to tell the whole world about me."

***

Later that evening, I wear my disguise cap and a thick jacket and throw pebbles at Emily's window. I feel like a teenage kid sneaking out from my house to get drunk, but what can I say? I miss her.

She opens the window and scans outside. I put my finger to my lips. Emily waves then disappears to open the front door and welcomes me with kisses.

After we creep inside her bedroom, she locks the door and wraps her arms around me. "Thank you for coming to see me."

We lie down on the bed underneath the blanket and cuddle.

"You're sure your dad won't hear us?"

"He's asleep, and he's half deaf." She chuckles, rubbing her feet against mine.

I feel so light when she's around, and although I'm much older than Emily, she makes me feel safe. We make love, and I never get tired of looking at her face or feeling her touch, her kisses.

Moments later, we are glued to the TV as Chuck's show airs.

"Since when does she wear yellow?"

"Yellow is a shout for sympathy," Emily says.

Liv's hair is swept to the side like she hasn't combed it. Dark circles underneath her eyes don't match the false stare she has at the camera.

"Mrs. Walters, on a scale of one to ten, how would you rate your marriage?" Chuck addresses Liv then faces the camera.

"I would say our marriage was pretty fair. Like any normal couple, we had our ups and downs."

"Oh please," I say.

"Would you rate that a five or above five?"

"Perhaps a seven or better yet an eight." She faces the camera. "David and I had our share of chores. He worked from home while I'm an ICU nurse. We may be very different, but he was my Ying and I his Yang."

I shake my head.

Chuck smiles. "I understand you were college sweethearts."

She smiles too. "Yes, and we still write each other letters. I've kept them all."

"Tell us about the night when he fell into a coma."

Liv sheds a tear and chokes up. "David came home that evening in a drunk rage. He said he was leaving me." She wipes her face.

"Bull shit," I raise my voice.

Emily hushes me.

"I told him we need to work things out and that divorce is not the solution…"

Chuck hands her a glass of water while the audience listens intently.

"But he was furious and didn't want to listen. He told me he didn't love me anymore and was leaving me for a younger woman."

The audience shouted, "Boo."

Chuck signals for them to be quiet. "And how did you feel?"

"Hurt, betrayed, and anything you can think of. I asked myself where did I go wrong. Was I not a good wife?"

"And where did you think you went *wrong?*"

After a long pause, Liv said, "I feel like I never appreciated David."

"A man needs to be constantly reminded of how much his wife appreciates him," Chuck says.

Liv crosses her legs and takes a sip of her water. "Yes, and I neglected him at times due to our busy schedules."

"When did this happen?" Chuck asks. "We'll hear the answer after the commercial break."

Emily glances at me. "Boy, she's good. Is what she said true?"

"Yes, but that doesn't change anything. She manipulated me into being her object of desire. I gave her everything she wanted, and as long as she was happy, I didn't complain." I hold her hands. "But it was all one-sided. She was selfish, and she's not capable of love."

The show comes back on air, and we see a more composed Liv, her shoulders now relaxed.

"As you were saying, Mrs. Walters..."

"Yes. This started about six years ago when we were trying to have a baby. Both of us were so focused on getting pregnant that we forgot about ourselves."

"Do you think if you had a child, this would change everything?"

She fondles her hair. "I've always wanted to have a child. I didn't grow up in a normal home, and I feel being a mother to a child would be the most precious gift to me."

"And so after you tried to convince your husband not to leave you, what happened?"

A thin line formed her lips. "He got angrier and pushed me against the wall."

"Oh no." Chuck opens his mouth wide. "Has he been violent to you before?"

"Only a few times, but this time, he was out of control. I tried calming him down, but he wouldn't listen, and the next thing I knew, he collapsed on the floor. I couldn't believe what I just saw. I called 911. The doctors told me slipped into a coma. The blood tests indicated a combination of drugs mixed with alcohol." She dabs her cheek with a tissue.

Emily pinches me. "Do you realize America is watching this now?"

"It'll be fine. I have a plan."

"And now, the love of your life, the man you took care of, has vanished," Chuck says.

"Yes, and this is why I'm pleading to all of you, if you see David..." A picture of me flashes through the screen. "Please tell him to come home."

"If David is watching right now, which I hope he is, what do you wish to tell him?"

Straightening her shoulders, Liv faces the camera. "David, if you're watching, I'm sorry I failed you, for hurting you. I love you. I need you. Please come home."

"Bravo!" I clap my hands. "Congratulations, Olivia Walters. You make America proud to have citizens like you."

Emily shuts off the TV and leans her head on my shoulder. "What is your plan?"

"I'm going to fake my own death."

"What?" Emily jerks away.

"Yup. But first, I need to ask you a favor."

She raises her eyebrows.

"Your bar makes the best burgers I've tasted and I'm really craving one."

Emily bursts into laughter, and seeing her dimples lifts my spirit.

I need to win the game because Emily is worth fighting for.

Day 15

Liv

I'm still flushed from my performance. Adrenaline surges inside me, and the audience gives a mighty applaud and takes turns embracing me. Chuck extends a heartfelt thanks for the exclusive interview, and I shed a tear, pretending to be sincere.

Back at home, I toss my sandals on the floor and lie on my bed. There are three messages from my mother-in-law. Diana is worried sick. A smile plays on my lips. If she comes here, I can avoid Aiden all together.

I punch in her number. She picks up right away and rattles on how concerned she is about her son.

"Mom." I begin to sob. "Yes, I'm frantic too." Wilma jumps up the bed sniffing David's pillow. She misses him too. "Can you come here and stay with me? I can't bear to be alone during this time."

"I'm taking the next flight out. You hang in there."

As soon as I end the conversation, Aiden calls me again.

"What do you want?" I can't hide my annoyance.

"Just so you're aware, Emily keeps avoiding my calls. I think she's with David."

Anger pokes me in the inside. "What?"

"That sure got your attention. Quite the performance you made today. Do you mind telling me your plans?"

"Do you expect me to be with someone who blackmails me?"

"Don't be so judgmental. Have you forgotten how you tried to kill your husband?" he mocks.

"You have no proof of that."

"I can show them recordings of you asking me to fuck Emily's brains off."

A cold shiver runs through my spine, and I'm now convinced I should get rid of Aiden. "What is it that you want?"

"Like I said, fifty thousand, and once you kill him, I'll need the rest of it."

"All right. Pick up the check now."

"That's my girl. I'll be there in two hours."

Phone gripped against my chest, I ask myself what am I going to do with him? I stare at the stack of cards from the nurses I work with in the hospital, all offering their encouragement and smile. *Being a nurse has its perks.*

***

My fellow nurses greet me at the hospital and are surprised that I'm back to work.

Tia, the head nurse, pulls me toward the corner. "I heard what happened," she whispers. "Is there anything we can do to help?"

"The detectives are trying their best to find David. I came here because I needed to get away from it all." I dab my cheeks. "I won't stay long though."

"Sure. I'm here if you need me." She gives me a tight hug.

When nobody is looking, I slip into the supply room and approach the syringe cabinet. I spot the syringes and bury them inside my purse. Drawers opened, I find potassium chloride and add it inside my bag.

I'm back making my rounds where I do small talk with each of the nurses. They extend comforting words and offer their support. The nurses respect how much I value my privacy, but they make it clear to me they are a phone call away if I need them.

***

Back at home, my mother-in-law sends me a text. She'll be taking the red eye flight that evening.

My doorbell rings, and wearing a black satin robe laced with perfume, I welcome Aiden.

He nuzzles my neck and steps inside. "Boy, I missed you." Aiden grabs me by the waist and kisses me.

"I missed you too." I escort him upstairs.

"Fine place you got here." From behind, he follows me. "Do you have my money?"

"I do." Tracing my fingers on his arms, I add, "But I want you first." My robe slips to the floor, revealing my naked body.

He beams then pushes me to the bed and kisses my neck.

I move back and lie on my pillow, my hand reaching for the syringe underneath. He continues to kiss me. My bare chest exposed, he rubs me with his frolicking hands and licks down my body. I moan and pull him up so I can kiss him, but Aiden insists on going down. Wiggling my toes, I can't lose control, but I really do want him.

He spreads my thighs and bends his head on my cherry. I don't know if I can kill him, but he *is* a distraction to my plan. I enjoy the last moments of him eating me till he moves up and kisses me hard and thrusts inside me.

"Yes," I moan.

Counting till ten, I reach for the syringe underneath my pillow and plunge it directly on Aiden's neck. I push all the potassium chloride into him. He stares at me with eyes wide. I pull my body away from him and push him so he can lie flat.

"What did you do to me?" He gasps for air.

I lean on top of him and whisper into his ear, "There was no need for me to do this, Aiden. If only you didn't blackmail me, none of this would have happened."

"Liv!" His body freezes, and his eyes become still.

"Nobody will know. It will look like you had a heart attack."

Aiden struggles to say something, but he releases his last breath, his eyes still open.

I shut his eyes. Now I need to dispose of Aiden's body. Shit! I dash to the bathroom and take fresh towels with water and soap then scrub his groin, mouth, and body.

In a hurry, I burn the syringe, erasing any trace of potassium chloride, pick up the phone and call Christopher. "I need you to come here now."

It only takes twenty minutes for Christopher to arrive, and he's dumbfounded when he spots Aiden dead in my bed.

Pacing around the room, I raise my hands in the air. "I met him on the cruise. He helped me forget about my situation."

"No wonder he looked familiar," Christopher says.

"I'm sorry I didn't tell you, but I need your help now."

"We need to call 911."

"Christopher, you know I can't say I was having an affair. Not with my situation," I plead.

Beads of moisture form on Christopher's forehead. "Gosh, Liv, what on earth did you get yourself into?"

"We need to make it appear that he was your lover."

"My lover?" Christopher rests his hands on his chest.

"Yes, please, Christopher. This is the biggest favor I'm going to ask you. And you're going to tell them he passed out while you were making love in my bedroom."

"Whoa, hold on." He jerks away. "Are you crazy?"

"Please, Christopher. It's not like I killed him. He died while we were having—"

He cuts me off. "I don't know how I'm going to ever sleep again."

"I owe you one." I glance at my watch, relieved it's only been thirty minutes since the event happened and it's nice to have a best friend handy when you need him.

***

What a day! The paramedics come and collect Aiden. Christopher is sobbing, and I'm there to console him while they ask questions. They want information about his immediate family, but Christopher can offer none. He explains he met Aiden in a casual encounter, and this was their first date.

"I don't know how I will explain this to Patrick," Christopher says before bidding me goodbye.

I don't offer a solution, glad I've gotten rid of Aiden. *My next goal is to purge Emily.*

Day 15

David

I'm so glad I spent time with Emily last night. It convinced me all the more that she's the woman for me and how much I want to move forward with my life.

Mark shows up at my motel room with food, clothes, and supplies.

"Thanks, bud! I don't know what I'd do without you." I escort him inside and inspect to see if anyone trailed him.

"Don't worry. Nobody followed me." He plops himself on the chair.

I lock the door and turn on the TV. "Why can't I watch something where my face is not displayed on the screen? It's insane."

"This has to end soon, David."

"It will. Have you thought about my plan?"

He folds his arms. "How are you going to pull this off?"

After removing my grimy shirt, I replace it with a fresh clean one. "I'm going to dab my blood on this shirt and you're going to dump it a few miles outside my house so someone can see it."

"Are you fucking kidding me? You'll need a lot of blood for that."

Removing the contents from the bag, I apply the latex gloves. I remove the bread knife. "This should do it."

"There's still no body."

"That's precisely it. I'm going to plant this knife in our dumpster when Liv's out. Once you dump the shirt, I'll send an anonymous tip to the detective handling the case. They'll find the shirt and then go search the house."

"Whoa, whoa, this is getting too complicated. When do you plan to do this?"

"Now. You'll need to help me scrape some skin so I can get enough blood."

Mark raises his hands in the air. "I'm not scraping anything. I'll take care of dumping your shirt."

"Okay, but I need you to get Liv out of the house so I can do this fast."

Mark agrees and bids me goodbye.

I don't recommend anyone scraping his skin. Opting for the back of my arm near my elbow, God knows how much I yelled, but I'm able to get enough blood to soak a shirt. I tuck the bread knife inside a hand towel. The garbage collectors won't come for another five days so we're safe.

Two tablets of Tylenol don't dissolve the pain throbbing from my arm. Maybe I'm crazy to do this, but my determination keeps me going. I'd love to see the look on Liv's face when she gets the call or when the news flashes, "Bloody shirt of Olivia Walters' husband found…"

The phone rings, and I'm eager to speak to Mark.

Emily pants. "I can't take this anymore. Aiden keeps texting me that if I don't come and see him tomorrow, he'll threaten to tell the cops I'm the woman you had an affair with. He wants to take me to his cabin."

I sigh. "They're going to find out sooner or later."

"I don't want this exposure. My dad's going to hate me, and I'll have cops coming to my house. I don't want to deal with this."

She's right. She didn't deserve this pressure. "Tell Aiden you'll meet with him in a public place, but not his cabin."

"He can always put a gun on my head and try to kill me if I don't comply to his demands."

She's right again. Boy, is she smart. "Honey, give me an hour. I need to think this through. I promise I won't disappoint you."

The clock is ticking and still no call from Mark. Finally, after fifteen minutes, the phone rings. "It's done." He hangs up.

Good, the shirt now rests in an alley two blocks from my house.

After I put on my cap, hooded jacket, and gloves, I barge out the door. A cold shiver runs through my spine as I tiptoe to my house. I remind myself I'm just an ordinary person walking around. Nobody should notice me, but I keep my eyes open. It's seven o'clock, and people are inside having dinner.

I'm fast approaching my house, and the lights are on. Liv's inside for sure. Taking two more steps, I dump the paper bag with its contents inside the dumpster. Using Liv's old cell phone, I send an email to the detective from an alias email about the tip. Then I smash the cell phone and dump it in the trash as well.

Liv will get what she deserves.

Day 16

David

I'm so busy surfing channels to see if there's anything on the news I forget to call Emily back until the next morning.

She picks up after one ring. "You promised to call me in an hour last night."

"Sorry." I tell her about what happened, still watching TV. "Is Aiden bugging you?"

"He stopped when I told him I want to meet him at a public place."

The news flashes an announcement.

"Turn on your TV to channel five. Let me call you back."

Two cops drag Liv outside as the reporter announces, "We are now outside Olivia Walters' house where they found a bloody knife inside her garbage bin." The camera zooms in on the garbage can. "Earlier today, the police also found a bloody shirt two blocks from the Walters' house."

"Woohoo. Bitch."

The reporter inches toward Liv. "What can you say about these developments?"

Liv yells, "You need to ask David's girlfriend, Emily Scott. She should know."

Fuck! Fuck! Fuck!

The cops push her inside the car, but she's still shouting. "Stop treating me like I'm a murderer. There's no body."

The camera focuses on the crowd and then on a woman crying.

Mom?

"David, I hope you're alive. Please come home," she pleads.

I turn off the TV and lie on my bed. Guilt showers upon me. I wish my mom never would have seen this. *Mom and Emily, the two most important women in my life are damaged now. I will do anything and everything to make my life normal again.*

Day 16

Liv

I'm inside a hot cell, fuming while waiting for the results of the DNA from the shirt and knife. How could David do this to me? It's my fault for getting distracted with Aiden. I freaked out when the cops came to the house, presuming it was because of Aiden, and it turned out to be this. But this time, they need to focus on Emily. Where is my fucking lawyer? They can't just fuck with me here. *I'm going to get you for this, David.*

As I pace around the cell like a caged animal, I device a plan. David is playing with me and intends to twist my mind. I need to be on guard and keep my aces hidden.

The guard approaches the cell with Detective Reed behind him.

"Where's my lawyer?" I ask.

The guard unlocks the bolt.

"You're free to go," Detective Reeds says.

I'm taken aback but don't show it.

Detective Reed escorts me outside. "We didn't find any other DNA aside from David's on his shirt."

"Thank God!"

"Yes, and there's nothing in your house. Do you think David is still alive? Does he have any enemies? Who do you think would do this to David? To you?"

I face her. "You need to look into Emily Scott. She should know about David's whereabouts."

"And why didn't you mention her before?"

I avert my gaze to the ground. "My husband was having an affair. It's painful for me to bring it up."

She doesn't flinch.

"C'mon. You're the detective here. You need to get to the bottom of this," I say, raising my voice.

***

I'm glad to be home, but that doesn't keep me from planning my next move.

My mother-in-law comes running to me from the kitchen. "I'm so glad you're home. I can't believe David would disappear like that. He loves you, and I hope he's okay."

I frown. "I'm sorry, Mom. I need to rest."

"Wait. There's someone in the kitchen who needs to see you. She said she's an old friend of yours."

My head is spinning, and all I want to do is curl up in bed and sleep. "Who is she?"

A tall, slim woman with long auburn hair pops out from the kitchen. "Hello, Olivia."

My heart stops. Where have I seen her before?

My mother-in-law excuses herself and heads to her bedroom.

The lady approaches me. "I'm Ruby, Aiden's sister."

I freeze, remembering the woman Aiden was arguing with in Rome. How the hell did she find me? "I'm so sorry for your loss."

Her lips form a thin line. "Aiden told me about you. He even sent photos." She's starting to shout.

My gaze shifts to my mother-in-law's bedroom, hoping she doesn't hear us. "Can I offer you some tea, coffee?" I fumble for words.

Her eyes spell anger. "I only need an explanation. I read the police report, and it said Aiden had a heart attack after having sex with a gay man in your house." She points a finger at me. "Aiden is not gay. I will get to the bottom of this."

Raising my hands in the air, I say, "Aiden was a good man, but I guess you didn't know that side to him."

She folds her arms, as if she's not convinced about what I just told her. "I can guarantee you I will not stop investigating about what happened. I suspect you are a part of it."

I take a deep breath. "Are you threatening me?"

"Isn't it weird that your husband is missing and now Aiden is dead?"

I approach the front door. "Please get out of my house!"

She marches outside. "I will return once I have evidence you killed my brother."

"I hope to never see your face again."

After she leaves, I lean my back against the door. This isn't happening. I need to learn how to multitask and prioritize how to better handle my enemies. *Ruby is another weed that needs to be mowed.*

Day 17

David

Emily isn't taking any of my calls. I tried to protect her, but now she's involved too deep.

Next, I call Mark.

"Dude." He talks like he's had five cups of coffee. "You can't keep calling me. I'm afraid they'll tap my phone."

"Relax." I raise my legs onto the table. "Would you be able to check on Emily? She isn't returning my calls, and I'm worried the press and detectives are bothering her."

"How is this going to end, David? Why don't you just tell the police the truth? Liv tried to kill you."

I pause. Mark is right. This isn't a game, and people I love are getting hurt. "Will the cops believe me? It's my word against hers."

"You have to try, David. This is going too far now."

"Do you think you can get Emily and I fake passports?"

"Are you fucking kidding me?" Mark yells. "Why do you want to live like a fugitive when you're not? And what makes you think Emily will do this for you?"

Why am I being a pussy? Why am I so afraid of Liv? "You don't know what Liv is capable off, Mark. She'll come to you when you're not looking. She's already tried that. I need to get this right."

Mark sighs. "Then whatever it is you need to do, don't waste time."

I dash to the bathroom, remove my bandage, and eye my wound. Still fresh. Definitely can't waste time. How long can I stay in the motel without running out of money? "I won't. Please check on Emily for me."

***

I'm digging through the old files at the library with a cap and glasses on, hoping nobody recognizes me. I remember a story Liv told me about how her adoptive parents died when she was sixteen. She said there was a fire, and she was the only one who survived.

The news displayed that in 1998 there was a fire in Fresno, California. As I narrow down the search, a clipping pops up and displays the story of a young Olivia and her dead adoptive parents. I read the article and cover my mouth. The suspicion? Arson by Liv. The other sites reveal the same implication. Just as I expected, Liv must have convinced everyone she was innocent.

The article also reveals Liv suffered from post-traumatic stress and was undergoing therapy. Liv never exposed strange behavior when we were dating.

I print the news clippings, scan them, and create an alias email. After typing in Detective Reed's email, I write, "How well do you know Olivia Walters?" then attach the scanned files. Perhaps she already has it, but better to send it anyway. *Liv can't run away from the truth.*

Day 17

Liv

My mother-in-law doesn't stop blabbering about how much she misses David while I slice the onions for our dinner that evening.

My chopping gets more rapid, matching my heart rate. "There are things you don't know about your son. He cheated on me."

"Do you have proof of that? Maybe it's just hearsay."

Heaving a sigh, I dash upstairs to the box where I kept our love letters and pluck David's journal. I rush downstairs and show it to her.

She reads the title, and her eyes fill with mist. "I thought you guys were happy."

Happiness seems to be overrated nowadays. There's a price to pay for it.

The doorbell rings, intruding our chat.

"I'll get it," she says.

Carrying my chopping knife, I follow her to the front door. "Let me." I take a peek on the peephole and spot Christopher outside.

Opening the door wide, I greet him.

His mouth carves into a line. "Hello, Diana." He nods to my mother-in law then faces me. "I need to speak with you." His gaze darts to my knife.

Diana seems to sense the tension between us so she excuses herself. Christopher follows me to the kitchen.

"Can I offer you anything?" I set the knife on the chopping board, open the refrigerator, pull out a pitcher of lemonade, and set it on the counter.

"Patrick broke up with me."

A sigh escapes from my lips. The bad news keeps coming, and I can't seem to take it anymore. "I'm so sorry." I wrap my arms around him.

He removes my hands. "That's not all. Aiden's sister came to see me."

After pouring two glasses of lemonade, I hand Christopher his drink.

He ignores my gesture and raises his voice. "You don't know how serious this is, Liv."

I've never seen Christopher angry. In our years of friendship, not once did we fight.

"I'm sorry."

"Sorry is not going to remove the stain of lies you've implicated on me so you better start talking."

I knock down my glass, and it shatters to the ground.

Christopher is unmoved. "If you don't tell me what happened, I will go to the police and tell them you asked me to lie for you."

"Please." I gesture, my hand in the air.

The odds are going against me and I need to work them to my benefit.

Day 18

David

I'm lying on my stomach with my eyes closed. Barely slept last night. My wound is healing slowly, but I can't seem to find a way out from my situation. Am I a coward for not confronting this head on?

A tap on the window intrudes my thoughts. My throat constricts as I bolt upright and peep outside the window.

My heart sinks in relief when I spot Emily outside. I drag her inside then check to see if anybody followed her. *Clear.*

She wraps her arms around me, and we don't say a word.

When Emily releases from our embrace, she plops into the bed, a pensive look on her face.

"I thought I'd never see you again." The thought of that is enough to drive me insane.

"I'm sorry. I needed to get away from it all. If it's not the detectives hounding me, it's the press."

I sit beside her and pull her against my chest. "Your dad must be so pissed off."

Her eyes light up. "If there's any consolation, the bar is always full."

We both share a laugh and tickle each other like little kids.

After giggling and goofing around, Emily cups my face in her hand. "I never got to show you the mural."

"Why don't we go now?"

The smile on her face is replaced by sorrow. "I'm sorry, David. I don't think I can see you no more."

My heart sinks like a deflated balloon. "Are you breaking up with me?"

Covering her face with both hands, she weeps. "I love you, but this is just too much for me."

I open my mouth, wishing I could erase the wounds from her heart. There's not one thing I can promise her. In shame, I bow my head.

"Dad and I thought it would be best that I move east with my aunt, my mom's sister," she manages to get out between sobs. "I came here to say goodbye."

A dagger stabs my heart. My wife tried to kill me, and now the woman I truly love is leaving me. I hate myself for being such a coward.

She rises and heads for the door.

"Emily."

Raising one hand in the air, she blurts out, "Don't bother. There's no guarantees."

"You know I love you," I plead, but it's like shooting empty bullets in the dark.

"The fear you have for your wife is more powerful than the love you have for me." Emily closes the door behind her, and she's gone like a wisp of smoke.

**

A cold gust of wind brushes through my cheeks as I finger the mural Emily made. I can taste the tears she shed while painting me when I was unconscious.

I have to fight for Emily.

Day 18

Liv

Voices whisper as my head throbs. Opening my eyes, I spot Diana and Christopher chatting and realize I'm at the hospital. The last thing I remember is Christopher threatening to tell the police about my affair with Aiden. Without hesitation, I collapse to the floor, my head landing on the broken glass.

My plan worked, and if I have to continue to lie and pretend, I will to save myself.

"Where am I?"

Diana rushes to my side. "Sweetie, it's okay. You're all right."

"Who are you?" I push her away, my gaze darting to Christopher. "Who is he?"

They exchange glances.

Diana speaks up. "Liv, I'm your mother-in-law, remember?"

"Get away from me!" I yell. "My name is Red."

A nurse comes rushing in. "What's going on?"

"These people are conspiring against me. Who are they?" I wrap my arms around my legs as if I'm frightened.

The nurse tries to pacify me. "Mrs. Walters, you're at the hospital. You had a bad fall, and your mother-in-law and best friend brought you here."

"I'm married? Where is my husband?"

Diana bows her head down.

The nurse purses her lips. "You need to rest." She signals them both to leave the room.

I spot the doctor approach them outside and read his lips as he says, "She could be suffering from post-traumatic stress disorder. After all she's been through, she'll need your support."

Great, my plan seems to be working. As long as I play my cards right, they have no choice but to leave me in peace. *Buying time equals temporary peace.*

Day 19

David

I can't believe Emily is gone, but I promise to come back for her. This will be over soon.

As I microwave frozen pasta, I channel-surf, hoping to get some update on the news. Looks like Liv came home. I need to do something bigger to startle her.

Liv's face flashes on the screen. I turn up the volume to listen to the reporter.

"A leak has informed us Olivia Walters is now in the hospital due to post-traumatic stress disorder."

Really, Liv? Couldn't you think of something better?

An image of a man appears on the screen as the reporter continues, "Aiden Frascone suffered from a heart attack after extreme lovemaking with Olivia Walters' best friend, Christopher Harris at her house." An image of Christopher is displayed on the screen. "Mrs. Walters' refuses to comment as she's in the hospital resting now."

Oh my God. Aiden's dead? How can these fuckers not put two and two together? She killed him, and now she's dragging in Christopher. Oh, Liv, do you see how many people you've involved in your scheme? If only you just let me go.

"In the meantime, David Walters is nowhere to be found."

The camera shifts its focus to a woman.

"We have here with us Ruby Frascone, Aiden's sister."

Ruby faces the camera. "My family and I are devastated about my brother's death, but we request you give us our privacy to mourn him." She curls her lip like she wants to share more information but doesn't.

The reporter concludes the segment.

Wow! I don't know how Liv is going to escape this. That's most likely why she's succumbed to her so-called PTSD.

***

I'm at the library to check my alias email. Detective Reed has responded to my email.

Would you like to meet? I will protect you.

I'm tempted to respond, but I need to think this through. *There's no way Liv will get away with this.*

Day 19

Liv

For the first time, I'm able to sleep through the night with the Valium they prescribed me. Each time my mother-in law or Christopher comes near me, I fake agitation so the doctor advises them to come back in a few days.

For once, I have peace and quiet. I need to plot out my next point of action. David is still missing, and Emily is still out there. Ruby is plotting against me, and I'm sure David is aware I'm in the hospital. But for now, we're even. *You have to play this smart, David. I will find you.*

I shut my eyes and sleep, the luxury I've missed the most.

Day 20

David

If I'm doing the math right, there are ten more days before Liv finishes her thirty-day wisdom project, which means ten more days till this nightmare is over. I wish I can call Emily and ask her to wait those ten days. I can live anywhere with Emily and not to mention my job. I have savings, but I can't touch them, which is why I think I'm going to see Liv and strike a deal with her.

Today, I'm going to email the detective from my motel room so she knows I've been here all along. Then I'm going to go see Liv in the hospital and work something out. But I can't do this alone, which is why I have a backup plan.

Ruby.

***

Ruby sits on the bench of the baseball field of Carfeld high school. We both agreed to meet at a public place where people won't notice us. I recognize her—the tall, slim, attractive lady on the news—as she pretends to watch the baseball practice.

Approaching her, I blurt out, "The kids should be here soon." The code we made up.

Lifting her head toward my direction, she nods and rises from the bench. We pace around the field, pretending to watch the high school boys practicing.

"So, it really is you?" She studies me from the rims of her glasses.

"Yep. Very much alive."

She turns to see if anyone is watching and murmurs, "Potassium chloride."

"What about it?"

"That's what she injected on Aiden," she mumbles.

"And couldn't they trace it in his blood test?"

"Aiden suffered from renal failure. He was asymptomatic and healthy, but people with that disease contain high potassium levels in their blood, which is why the autopsy was consistent with the story of Aiden dying from a heart attack. She killed my brother and left no marks."

"Liv's a nurse. Look what she did with me." I stroll along the field beside her, feeling sorry for Ruby's loss and glad she's helping me.

She stops in her tracks then faces me. "So what are you going to do?"

I tell her my plan, and that if all doesn't work in ten days, then she can come in the picture and do what she has to do. "I'll tell her she should just kill me on my own terms since I'm slowly dying, that a brain tumor manifested after my coma. I'll convince her I'll be a liability, and my life insurance will take care of her. I'll record her and get her to admit she killed Aiden and that she tried to kill me. We'll put hidden cameras in the house so you can send the footage to the cops."

"You're going to make a deal with the devil?"

"Pretty much."

She shakes her head. "It's not that simple, especially since she wants you."

I grin. "Maybe you know someone who can give you a fake doctor's note indicating I have a brain tumor. Then I'll throw the question back at her. Why would she want to spend all her years taking care of an unhealthy person like me? The medical bills would spike, and we would be miserable. She'll make more money from the life insurance. I'll tell her I don't want to wait till the tumor consumes me."

Her eyes beam, and her body shakes in excitement. "Boy, you're good."

"Strategy." I avert my gaze to the baseball soaring in the sky.

"How long will this take?"

I look at her straight in the eye. "Ten days. That's all I ask."

"As a matter of fact, I have a good friend who can write a fake doctor's note for you."

A grin plays on my lips. "I knew I could count on you."

***

Back at the motel, I pack my clothes and dispose my trash then send an email to Detective Reed. *I will need you to trust me first. Don't bother Olivia Walters for now. Give me ten days, and I promise you'll get to the bottom of this case.*

As soon as I send the email, I lay down on my bed, pretending to be unconscious again. It's only in this position where I can think straight. What if Liv says no? She can't. *Failure isn't an option. I have to coax her. She has to trust me again. I have to win her pity.*

Day 20

Liv

Although I slept peacefully last night, I can't stop thinking about David. Where did he go? Has something bad happen to him, or is he just faking this? Why can't he come home? Doesn't he love me anymore?

My mother-in-law pops in with a paper bag. "Good morning, Olivia. I hope you were able to get a good night sleep."

I stare at her with empty eyes. Although I pretend I don't remember her, I'm grateful she's taking care of Wilma our cat. The doctor has prohibited the detectives from bothering me during this time. So unless David comes home, I'll stay here.

"I brought your wedding album to help you remember David." She hands it to me.

I take it from her and flip through the pages. We had dreams and hopes for a beautiful life, and I believed David could help me erase my past. But I learned now that no matter how you try to forget, your past will always come to haunt you.

A wave of anxiety crashes on me. Closing my eyes, I hear the familiar voices I've tried to erase.

"You're stupid. I told you to lock the door," my foster mother said.

"I told you she was stupid," my foster father added. "Don't know why you agreed to keep her."

Stupid became such a common word, I couldn't count how many times they told me that.

She rolled her eyes then faced me. "Next time you do that, Olivia, you're sleeping in the barn."

I stared at them blankly.

"Did you hear what I said?" she yelled.

I didn't blink and cursed them under my breath. *Let's see who's stupid now.*

Later that evening, while they were sound asleep, I poured the house with gasoline, lighted a match, and rushed to the barn.

As the flames danced, I covered my ears, refusing to hear their wails, repeating, "Nobody calls me stupid," over and over again.

I continue to peruse the photo album then set it aside on the nightstand.

Diana removes David's Armani perfume and positions it near my nose. "They say scents can stimulate one's memory."

Shaking my head, I face the other direction. I have to give her credit for trying. No mother would want to lose their child and see their daughter-in-law not remember a thing.

The doctor knocks on the door and circles around my bed. "Good morning. How did you sleep last night?"

"I've had better days," I lie.

He nods. "I need to run some tests."

I start shaking. "I just want to rest."

"All right, you get some sleep." He eyes Diana and leaves the room.

Diana clears her throat. "Sweetie, you just need to let me know what you need. I'm not going anywhere."

Great, Diana replaced David.

What can I do that will make David come home? I can't lose him to that slut. Nobody comes between David and me. Maybe I can entice him. I have to give David what he wants. That's the only way he'll return to me.

But what does David really want? I want to be with David alone, so it would be best if Diana goes back home. Boy, I'm tired of her.

David is mine.

Day 21

David

At the crack of dawn, I march down the streets of San Francisco, leaving my sanctuary behind. Nobody knows my plan except for Ruby. I practiced stuttering, limping, and twitching all night and also didn't shower nor comb my hair. Wearing soiled clothes, I want to show Liv what a pathetic loser I am.

Although Liv is Ms. Fix-It and the woman who can take care of all, I'm going to prove to her the man she loves is unfixable, that she should just terminate me—an assisted suicide. I will be so needy she won't like it. She'll agree to my terms because if she can't have me, neither can Emily. She'll still win.

My body surges with adrenaline. The first thing I need is for my mother to leave. She can't see me like this. After wrestling with my thoughts, I decide my mother needs to be aware of my plan. I make a quick phone call to Ruby, and she agrees. My mother can stay with her while I fulfill my goal. Talk about a silver lining.

***

Nobody is in sight and Liv must be in the hospital. I want to surprise Mom and see her reaction. I miss her so much. The door creaks when I enter the house. Wilma wraps her tail around my legs and purrs.

"I missed you too." I draw in the familiar sounds and scents of my own home, but this time, I feel like a stranger. Heading to my office, I discover Liv has left everything alone. My computers are in the same place, and if the cops checked it, they wouldn't find anything but work stuff and the porn sites I browsed.

I back up all my files in USBs and think about what else can I bring with me when I'm gone. The house is filled with memories, and I can't wait till it's over.

Mom's usually an early bird and should be down in the kitchen soon.

I step inside our bedroom, smelling the faint traces of Liv's perfume. Checking the closet, I notice my clothes are still hanged like I never left. It only confirms Liv has been waiting for me.

What will Liv do without me? Will she survive prison? She'll find a way to manipulate somebody there for sure, but I'm no longer scared of her. My plan has to work. I hear footsteps and a shadow carrying a baseball bat approaches me.

"Mom, it's me, David."

The footsteps stop.

A prickle behind my neck stands. "Mom, did you hear what I said? It's me, David."

Coming out of the bedroom to get a closer look, my mom freezes. I burst into laughter, and we share a tight embrace.

Tears spill out from her eyes. "I thought you were dead."

I hold her hand against my chest. "No, Mom."

"Liv is in the hospital. She doesn't remember a thing. Perhaps she will remember you."

We walk toward the bed and sit down.

"Where were you, David?"

"Mom, I have so much to say, but what I'm about to tell you might scare you."

She covers her face with both hands. "Oh, David, I can't take any more tragedy."

I wrap my arms around her. "You have to trust me, Mom, but first of all, I need to know if I can trust you too." Narrating how it all began, I inform her about our failed marriage, to Emily, to my coma, Aiden, and my ultimate plan.

She covers her face. "Oh my gosh! How deceiving of her."

"Yes and I can't do this without you."

"What do you need me to do?"

I pace around the room, wanting to move my legs. "I need you to tell Liv you're going back to Boston and that she should go home so she can remember and rest. You have to convince the doctors she is ready to go home, that this will help her memory."

"I can do that."

"Insist she can't have any press or detectives bothering her," I add.

"I can't leave you here." Her eyes are red from crying.

"You will stay with Ruby, Aiden's sister. She'll help."

Mom weeps and gives me a tight hug. "I hope your plan works, David. I can't afford to lose you again."

"Everything will be fine."

I've gone this far. I need to finish this.

Day 21

Liv

The doctor provides me a release form when Diana pops in.

She greets both of us then eyes my bags. "You're leaving?"

Dr. Scholl beams. "I believe it will be safe for her to go home now. Tests are normal, and she needs to rest. It will help her remember. If any concerns should arise, please call me."

"Thank you, doctor," Diana says.

"Very well. Have a nice day."

Diana carries my other bag, and I'm surprised she didn't contest my plans.

"You look so lovely, Olivia." She clasps my hand. "I'm sure in time, you will remember."

I force a smile as we take a cab. Moments later, we arrive outside my house .

After we step out of the car, she stops. "Olivia, I know this may seem abrupt, but I need to go back to Boston."

"Boston?" I raise my eyebrows. Why the sudden rush?

"That's where I live. You'll be fine."

I nod, pretending to be grateful. "I'm sorry I don't remember you."

"I feel the solitude will be able to provide clarity." She steps back inside the cab.

I wave goodbye and stand in front of my doorstep. I'm home.

The door creaks when I enter, and Wilma jumps right at me. Finally, I can be alone. No Diana, Christopher, doctors or nurses to check on me. No detectives to interrogate me. I swirl on the tiles like a ballerina performing to her audience.

My house is neat and spotless. Diana kept everything in place. All I want to do is collapse in my bed and not think about anything. *Except David.*

Staggering up the stairs, I head straight to my bedroom and open the door. As I'm about to jump onto my bed, I freeze and blink my eyes. It can't be. Heart pounding, I approach the bed and look into his closed eyes. *David.*

I stare at him, thinking how pure he looks when sleeping. Nothing exposes the philandering husband in him. His beard is long, his clothes are soiled, and there is an unfamiliar stench about him, but I don't care. I want to shake him, wake him up, and ask him where the hell he's been, except peace transcends over me. *David is home. He came home. He loves me.*

Leaning my head on his chest, I listen to his heartbeat. No sooner do I feel his hand caress my cheek. Lifting my head, I face him, cupping his face in my hands. *David.*

He curls his lip. "L-L-iiii-v."

Oh no! What's wrong with him.

"David. You're home."

"Home," he repeats, taking deep breaths. "Ssssorrryyyy."

My throat thickens as I swallow hard. I can't bear to see him this way. "What happened to you, David? Where did you go? They found blood all over your shirt. Who did this to you?" I raise my voice, frantic. I have to protect him.

He squeezes my arms, but then his hands go limp. "Forgive me," he says with tears in his eyes. "I l-l-love youuuuu."

"I love you too." I kiss his hands, wanting to hear him lament. "We belong together."

"We do." He pulls his body upward as one of his eyelids droops down. "I'm ho-o-omme."

"Yes, and you're never going anywhere."

He holds me against his chest and closes his eyes. God, do I want to take care of this man.

Later that evening, we both wake up from a deep sleep. I'm amazed at how peaceful I feel for the first time in a long while, how in tune David and I still are. He tucks a strand of my hair away from my face and kisses me softly.

I press my cheeks on his face, wanting him to shower me with kisses. His eyes never leave mine as we gaze upon each other.

"Do you want me to cook something? Are you hungry? I can make some soup."

"Soup will be nice." He speaks slowly.

"Come with me to the kitchen." I take his hand.

He rises slowly, limping with one leg, back hunched. Leaning his arm against my shoulder, I lead him to the kitchen. David settles into a chair, and it's like old times when I would cook and he would stay with me in the kitchen.

All I have are Instant Ramen noodles, but the smile on David's face is something I can live for. We eat in silence, side by side, glued like velcro.

As I clear the dishes, David says, "Liv."

"Yes."

"I neeeeed to speak with you."

I straighten my shoulders. "What is it, David?"

He takes my hand and holds it tight. "I'm dying."

"No, you're not," I raise my voice, reminding myself it's my fault he's this way. Did I have to torture him to humble himself and prove how much he needed me, that he was nothing without me? I have no regrets. I try to justify my actions as Emily's face creeps inside my head.

"I came heeeeere to makkkkke amends," he whispers. "My daysssss are nummmmbered."

"What are you talking about?"

He removes a folded paper from inside his pocket and passes it to me. His reflexes have slowed down, he has a lost a dramatic amount of weight, and his skin is gray.

I read the paper, a doctor's note indicating a brain tumor and my body freezes. The events replay on my mind, and I wonder what life would be if that night were different. I face the other way as a grin plays on my lips. Now Emily can't have him. She wouldn't want him. David came home to be with me. He knows I'll take care of him.

Dabbing my cheeks, I face him. "This can't be, David."

"I cammmme herrrre to spend your birthhhhhday. This will be your last birthday we'll spennnnnnd together."

Right, my birthday is eight days away.

He continues, taking deep breaths, "I wannnnnt to make it special. Just youuuuu and I. Please don't tell anyone including my mother I'm home yet. I want to be with you."

I don't want him to exert any effort, but he insists.

"I regret every momennnnnnt I had with her. I realized how much you meannnnn to me. She is nothing comparedddd to you."

I squeeze his hands, my heart skipping a beat. "Let's forget about everything, David. We can start over, somewhere new."

"I don't have much time," he says. "I need you to do something for me."

"Anything." He has my full attention.

"I want to die in my own terms." His lips form a line.

"David."

"I need to die with dignity, and I want you to do it for me. I can't wait till the tumor consumes me."

"You're asking me to kill you," I choke, but then I remember I almost did that. However, back then, it was a crime of passion. *This is something different.*

"Assisted suicide," he says. "Nobody will know except you and I. It will be our secret."

My heart pounds, and my palms sweat. Never did I think my husband would ask me to do such a thing.

"Think about it, Liv. I will be a liability to you. You can use the insurance money, and I will die peacefully in your arms."

I take a deep breath. My husband is serious about this, and his humility touches me. I owe him my life, and although I hate to see him go, I say in a hushed tone, "Yes."

He weeps. "Thank you."

I clear my throat. "When do you want to die?"

"The day after your birthday."

My body freezes, bursting into tears then laughter. "Yes, I will do it for you."

Crazy as it sounds, but I just received validation that my husband will sacrifice everything for me.

Day 22

David

My plan worked. Liv agreed to fulfill my goal. I couldn't help notice how attentive she is to me, the extra care of cooking, cuddling, and making my life comfortable.

Liv sets the breakfast tray in bed. "Good morning, honey."

I force a smile as she leans over to kiss me.

"It's a beautiful day." She opens the curtains. "It's too bad we're indoors."

Averting my gaze to the food, I pop some bacon into my mouth. "Thanks for making breakfast. You don't have to give me special treatment." I twirl my fork on the scrambled eggs. "But I'm not complaining."

Wiping my mouth with a paper napkin, Liv says, "You know how much I love *taking care* of you."

As I munch on my food, Liv watches me. I hope she hasn't thought of poisoning me. "What?"

"What?" She shrugs.

"You're staring at me."

She smiles then removes the tray and exits the room. When she returns, she says, "I think you should get a second opinion."

"What do you mean?"

"You need to see another doctor."

"For God's sake, I've had enough of doctors. The headaches are terrible, my potassium levels are up, but with you, I forget I'm sick. I want to make our last days together special."

Folding her arms, she leans her body against the wall. "You seem to be getting better." She pulls a mirror inside her nightstand and shows it to me. "Take a look at yourself. When you arrived here, your skin was gray. You stuttered and could barely walk. Today, your cheeks are flushed. You're glowing, and I haven't heard you stammer since."

Shit! She's so damn observant. "That's because I'm trying to please you." I look away, gearing myself to cry. "I don't want you to remember me as a pathetic weak husband."

"Don't even think that." She dashes to my side and embraces me.

I squeeze her hand. "I promised you I was going to take you to the Eiffel Tower for your birthday, and I can't even do that."

She grips me tight. "That doesn't matter now. As long as we're together, I'll be fine."

We don't say a word as she lies close to me. She believes I don't have time left and have nothing to offer her. Does she love me that much?

Why did she become attracted to me in the first place? I'm just an average guy and probably boring in her standards. Have I met her needs? Perhaps the needs to control.

"Honey, I need to do some quick errands. Will be back soon."

I'm glad she's going to leave me alone in the house. I'm tired of pretending.

"Be careful," I say.

"Don't worry." She slips into our walk-in closet and reappears wearing a dark wig, sunglasses, and a hat. "How do I look?"

I drop my jaw and clap my hands. "I would never have recognized you."

She smirks then exits the room.

***

Ruby delivers the package at the back door. It's such a relief to know she has my back. "Hidden cameras for your bedroom, kitchen, and living room. I would advise you stay in the same place at all times."

"Are you sure you're not a detective?"

Ruby laughs. "I'm a journalist in Italy, but I dream of writing a psychological thriller. I think I already have a story." She grins.

"Well, I hope your story has a happy ending."

She pokes my chest. "That will be up to you."

I shrug, hoping my plan works. What's the worst thing that could ever happen? "How's my mom?"

"Anxious to get this over with."

I nod. "Tell her soon… and that I love her."

Ruby waves.

I need to be consistent and not allow Liv to be suspicious. As it is, Liv believes what I told her. *I'm confident I will have my happy ending.*

Day 22

Liv

I'm glad I left the house. David seems so clingy and needy, and I have to take a break. Perhaps a walk will clear my head so I take a stroll to the skate park where Emily painted a mural of David. As skaters swing by, I gaze at his face. What did Emily do to make David fall in love with her? She gave him attention. Treated him like a star—*a hero*.

I remember when David and I first met. We were both young, and I had treated him like a hero too. But just when I stopped paying attention to him, he went looking elsewhere. The same thing with Aiden. The minute I pulled away, he blackmailed me.

This is a game I need to win. David is asking me to do something for him. Will it benefit me? Without him, I will no longer be a wife. My life is meaningless, and there's nothing in this world anymore.

Perhaps we can do it sooner. Waiting will only get us depressed. Why is David prolonging it? There must be something he's not telling me. *I need to find out what.*

Day 23

David

Liv and I are in the kitchen drinking beer and laughing about the good old days. I never anticipated I would be sharing jokes with my psychopath wife.

"Do you remember that time you told me to buy you sanitary napkins?"

"Oh yes." She explodes into giggles. "And you ended up purchasing bladder control pads."

My cheeks are flamed from laughing. "I thought I learned my lesson the first time, but it happened again twice."

"Yes. That's why I decided to wear a tampon instead." She presses her lips against mine. "I want to ask you something." Her eyes are guarded.

"Sure."

"Why do we have to wait seven more days to pursue your plan?"

I circle around the breakfast nook and open the refrigerator to grab two more beers. "I want to celebrate your birthday."

"Who cares about my birthday?"

I set the beers on the countertop. "Am I such a liability that you want me dead now?"

She raises her hands in the air as if to pacify me. Something's not right. Liv's starting to analyze my judgment.

We don't say a word. Fear creeps inside me.

There's a loud knock in the front door. We exchange glances, and Liv signals for me to go upstairs. *Shit!* Who could be outside?

The knock continues as I dash up the stairs and lean my head against the hallway.

Liv opens the door. "Can I help you?"

I can't hear the other person's voice. My heart's pounding too loud. Fuck, who is it?

Suddenly, I hear the door close. I wait a few minutes, hoping Liv comes upstairs but she doesn't. My palms begin to sweat. Where are you, Liv? Fuck! What is going on?

My head spins and I try to calm my fears. Thank God Ruby advised me to put in a hidden camera. Why the hell did I trust my wife?

As the minutes swing by, I tiptoe down the stairs toward the unlocked front door. I approach the window, checking to see any sign of Liv. *Nada.*

Scrambling up the stairs, I grab my disposable cell phone underneath inside my office desk, and call Ruby.

She answers after one ring. "Are you okay?"

"Did you get that? Who was at the front door?"

Panting, she stutters, "Um... uh."

"Ruby, please. I need to know."

"Emily." She breathes out a sigh.

I freeze. *Emily.* Oh my fucking God! Why the hell did Emily have to come and ruin it? "Where did she take Liv? What did she say?"

"She didn't say a word. Liv shut the door."

This isn't getting easier for me. I cover my face. "Where would Emily take her? You gotta help me with this, Ruby. I can't go out of the house."

"Yes, you can. It's you who wanted to do this stupid plan instead of going directly to the police. What is it about Liv that scares you to death?"

"It's not as simple as you think."

"You are just like Liv," she says. "You're psychotic and crazy to pull this off. If it weren't for my brother, I wouldn't be helping you. I want justice more than you do. If you want to play your game, you should just work your marriage out. You two belong together."

I'm not used to a woman other than my wife giving me the earful, but Ruby is right. Why am I enjoying every minute of my game? What if she's also correct that I'm sick in the head? Why am I still so attached to Liv?

"I'm sorry you feel that way, but please don't give up on me. I need you to find out where Emily took her."

"You owe me big time," Ruby says, raising her voice.

"I owe you my life."

A heavy responsibility rests on my shoulder. *There's no way I can fail.*

Day 23

Liv

Right in front of me is my greatest nemesis. I always anticipated this day would come. Coming face to face with my enemy again only proves my day of reckoning. I still can't believe David replaced me for this tramp.

She stands there, plain as day—no makeup and sweats looking like a studious schoolgirl unworthy of stealing my husband. With bloodshot eyes, she appears like she wants to throw words at me. I cling to her arm and guide her down the road. We walk side-by-side, like two close friends. She seems to know where I'm taking her as we march down the street that leads to the skate park.

We approach the mural and stare at David's face.

I speak up first. "We both love the same man. What are we going to do about it?"

Her lips quiver. "He doesn't love you."

I face her, raising my eyebrows. "Define love."

She gathers her thoughts. "Love is about freedom, not control. It's pure and kind. Love is a sacrifice."

"Sacrifice?"

"Yes, *sacrifice*."

"So, tell me, Emily, why did you come to see me?"

"You know why." She yanks her arm away.

I shrug.

"I know your dirty little secret," she whispers, averting her gaze to the skaters.

"What are you going to do?" My lips form a line. "Call the cops?"

"Even better." She circles behind me and pushes me against the wall, my face touching David's. "I'm going to make you suffer."

My head throbs and I push back, but she escapes. I rest my hand on my head. *Bitch! I'll make sure she pays for all she has done to me.*

Day 24

David

Liv finally comes home after two hours.

"Where were you? Who was that at the door?" My anxiety is killing me. I told Emily to wait, but obviously she wanted to take matters in her own hands. She doesn't realize she's destroying my plans.

"It was that stupid detective. Why can't they just leave me alone?" Liv marches up the stairs as I follow from behind.

Why can't Liv tell me the truth?

I play along, sitting beside her as she sprawls on the bed. "What did she say?"

"She took me on a car ride to the motel you stayed at not far away."

My throat thickens. How could she possibly know this? I only told Emily, Mike, and Ruby about it. Something's not right.

She continues to rattle on. "She drove around the alley were they found your bloody shirt."

"And what did you tell her?"

"I pretended to be oblivious. I'm supposed to be grieving your disappearance, and I don't want to offer her any clues that you're home."

That was Liv, always composed, exuding grace under pressure.

"Didn't the doctors instruct them to not bother you?" I ask.

She strokes my arm, seemingly affectionate. "Oh, David, they will never stop bothering me, which is why we need to do this sooner rather than later."

She's right. I don't know why I keep prolonging this. With Emily in the picture, trouble is looming. I need to act fast.

"We need to call your mom at least and tell her you're alive. She calls every morning to see if there are any updates."

"Please," I beg. "I don't want my mother to see me this way. Let's think about it."

Liv is lying to me. *She's testing how far I will go, and I'm not giving in to her terms. We're going to do this my way.*

Day 24

Liv

There is a big problem. *Emily*. She's only going to make things worse. Perhaps I can strike a deal with her.

It's almost midnight, and David is fast asleep so I tiptoe downstairs and leave the house.

***

Emily, in her pajamas opens the door ajar. "What the hell are you doing here?"

I push it wide open. "To finish what you started yesterday."

"Really? You want to fight? Why don't we handle this like two adults and not play discreet."

"You're calling me discreet? You were sleeping with a married man." I barge inside her house.

"Which I didn't know until you told me." She takes me to the kitchen.

"Who's there?" a booming male voice from upstairs echoes.

Emily rolls her eyes. "It's okay, Dad. It's my friend. Go back to sleep."

The sound of footsteps permeates through the hall.

I study the countertops to see if there are any sharp objects Emily might use against me in case things get heated, but there are none.

Emily plops herself on a bar stool. "What can I do for you?"

I remain standing, not wanting to act like we're best friends scratching each other's back. "I have a proposal for you."

She leans her chin on both hands and looks me straight in the eye. "And what makes you think I would want to strike a deal with you?"

"If it will benefit you, then I'm positive you will agree."

Her expression doesn't change.

"We have one thing in common. *David.*"

"I couldn't have agreed more."

I sigh. "We both love him very much, and in a situation like this, people get hurt, but not if you play it smart."

"There's always a catch."

"Well..." I lick my lips, proud of myself for thinking of this idea. "As you know, they're looking for David and you obviously don't know where he is."

She doesn't say a word, her eyes still glued to me.

"And David is not going to come out unless he gets something in return, so why don't we make him win? We can do this together."

"What is this, some kind of game you play to twist my mind?"

"Will you freaking pay attention to me, Emily? As it is, the detectives are at my back and they keep harassing you. You are also seen as the marriage wrecker. Don't you want to turn that around and come out like the *hero*?"

She gives me dagger looks but doesn't object.

"If you want to clear your name, you gotta make this viral."

"Viral?"

"Yes. I want you to apologize to me on national TV that you are the reason David and I had problems in the first place. You are to blame for his escape and you're sorry."

"Are you fucking out of your mind? And what am I supposed to get out of this while I bloat your ego?"

I lean on the countertop and flash her a grin. "In return, I will make sure you have David."

"It's not up to you to decide what David wants. David wants me. He made that choice early on and you—"

"I can guarantee, Emily, you will never see David again, if you don't do this."

"Is that a threat?"

I raise my voice. "We both don't know where David *is*."

"And how do you know I don't know where he is?"

Is she that dumb?

"You wouldn't come looking for him if you knew." I dig inside my purse, pluck out a business card, and hand it over to her. "Call Chuck. He can squeeze you in live tomorrow. Everybody will love you, Emily. You will be the girl next door every man would want to have. They'll probably offer you a book deal, a movie too..."

Once her ego gets bloated and she receives all the attention, she won't have time for David nor will she care about him anymore. Then I can have David all for myself till he dies. I want David to die knowing I was the one who stuck with him till the end. David chose to come home to me, to his *wife*.

She doesn't even look at the card. "Don't think you can manipulate me like you do David."

"I don't need to convince you to do it." With that said, I head to the door and exit her house.

My ducks are forming a straight row.

Day 25

David

Liv and I are curl up in bed watching TV and eating popcorn. I don't remember the last time we did this.

She leans her head on my shoulder while we play footsies. As she surfs the channels, she stops at the Chuck Small's show. "Oh my God."

"What?" I squint my eyes to get a closer look. My heart leaps for a moment then deflates like a balloon with no air when I see Emily.

We exchange glances, and for a moment, I know she must have manipulated Emily to do this. There are more layers to Liv I don't know. How long can we continue playing this game? We might as well just kill each other.

Chuck introduces Emily, who doesn't stop touching her hair. Her navy blue dress adds a glow to her angelic face and her hair is neatly tucked around her ears.

"Today, we have with us the lady who refused to talk, who ran away from it all, but tonight, she gathered her courage to speak up about the missing David Walters. Good evening, Emily Scott."

Liv and I are glued to the TV as Emily responds, "Thank you for having me here, Chuck."

"Tell me, Emily, how did it feel to find out you were having an affair with a married man? Is it true that you never knew David happened to be married?"

The muscles on her neck tighten. How could she possibly do this? I hate Liv even more for pressuring Emily. Liv has a smirk spread all over her lips.

"That's very true."

"Why do you think he never told you he was married?"

She bows her head and waits a few seconds to answer. "Some people have reasons for not being honest. I don't want to presume why David chose not to tell me."

Liv flashes me a glance. "She's playing safe, isn't she?"

I ignore her question.

"Was it a serious affair?" he asks Emily.

"I'm not one to play around. I loved David. I still do even if…" She breaks down and sobs.

Chuck leans over and hands her a Kleenex box.

"Oh, c'mon." Liv scowls.

"Even if it's wrong," Emily blurts out.

"Yet you're here today to make amends."

"Yes. To the people I hurt the most." She faces the camera and swallows hard. "David's wife, Olivia Walters."

Liv rubs her hands and straightens her shoulders. This is her reigning moment.

A picture of Liv flashes to the screen.

"I never meant to hurt you. I don't want to take what's yours, and I'm truly sorry for what I've done."

Liv beams.

Chuck applauds, and so does the audience. "Not many people possess the humility you exude, Emily." He shifts slightly and addresses the crowds "As you know, Emily painted a mural of David Walters."

A photo of the mural pops up on the screen.

Liv's expression changes from delight to disgust.

"That was my way of honoring David and grieving for him. I may never see David again, but I will cherish the memories we shared. David, if you're watching, what we had was special, but you need to come home to your wife. That's where you belong."

"Bravo." Liv applauds and tosses the remote to the side. "That was quite a performance. " I excuse myself and storm out of the room and head to my office. My breathing turns rapid, and I form a fist and punch the wall. *God knows how much I want to kill Liv but for now, I need to breathe.*

Day 25

Liv

Heat permeates down my neck as I wash my hands. I'm so thrilled Emily took the bait. I can guarantee she'll forget about David once the press announces, *Girl next door becomes America's sweetheart.* Who needs David?

The bathroom door swings open, and David emerges with eyes cold as stone.

"Hi, honey, I'm almost done." I bend down and splash water on my face.

He doesn't say a word.

"What a show that was, right?"

My nose hits the sink. Ouch! Blood oozes from my nose. David yanks my hair and I yelp. My scalp is burning with pain.

"You really mapped this out, didn't you?" He spits on my neck.

Air escapes my lungs, and I know David could kill me right now. I have to show him I'm afraid, that I'm vulnerable. "If you let me speak, I'll tell you."

He pulls my hair even tighter, ripping some out. Blinding pain consumes me.

"Please, David," I plead. "I didn't want to tell you it was Emily who came here to the house. I didn't want you to get hurt."

David leans closer to my ear and yells, "Liar." He tugs my hair and yanks me to the other side of the bathroom which causes me to trip.

"Listen to me, David." I gain my balance. "Why would I want Emily to come out on national TV? What the hell will that do for me? She admitted she didn't know you were married, that she was sorry, that what she did was wrong, and that you need to come home to your wife. Don't you get it, David? She's using your disappearance to her advantage."

David just stares at me, eyes open wide.

"You're pretty naïve, you know that? You think a young girl like Emily doesn't want attention? I mean, why would she want to announce on national TV that she's sorry? From what I perceived of her, she's a private person."

"You don't know anything about her," David lashes out, but he releases my hair.

"I'm sure more than half of America loves her now. She showed them her vulnerability, like she did with you when she brought you to the skate

park and showed you her mural and told you her sad story." Beads of moisture stain my cheeks.

He smashes his hand against the wall. "How the hell do you know that?"

Straightening my shoulders, I look him straight in the eyes. "Because she told me. Let me guess. That's the day you fell in love with her."

David shakes his head and rubs his chin.

I can almost read his mind. He's doubting Emily. "She used you, David. Just watch. This won't be the first TV show Emily will do. Next thing you know, publishers will offer her a book deal with seven figures. I wouldn't be surprised if they make it into a movie."

David storms out of the bathroom, and I sigh in relief. I'm confident David believes everything I said. He'll realize that after all we've been through, I stuck it out with him. *Nobody loves David like I do. He belongs to me.*

Day 26

David

Setting aside the strong cup of coffee, I sit on the countertop. Liv and I didn't talk anymore last night. I swear I could have killed her, and for the first time, I saw fear in her eyes. Why did Emily have to do this? How could she tell Liv about that time in the skate park? Fuck. That was a defining moment between us. Did Emily just use me?

Liv comes down the stairs, wearing a gym outfit. "I'm going out for a run. I need to clear my head."

"Sure," I say, wanting her to leave me in peace.

"And after that, I'm going to join the search group."

"Search group?" I settle my mug on the sink.

Raising her eyebrows, she adds, "The one I organized when you went missing."

"Right."

She grabs the keys and smiles. "So do I look like a grieving wife?"

I force a smile. "You look beautiful."

As soon as Liv leaves, I dash to my office, reach underneath my desk where I hid my phone, and call Ruby.

"Did you get that on video?"

"I didn't have to. I saw Emily on TV as well."

I pace around the room like a hamster on wheels. "No, I meant after the show. In the bathroom."

Ruby breathes through the phone. "You know there's no hidden camera inside the bathroom."

Fuck! Fuck! Fuck! I slide my hands down my face in frustration as I narrate to Ruby what happened.

"I mean, how could Liv possibly know what Emily confided in me?"

"What can I say? You tend to attract psychotic women," Ruby says in a flat tone.

"Why does life have to be so complicated? I don't think I can push through with my plan." I raise my hands in the air.

"Really? You want to go back to being a coward again?"

I can't find a way out of my situation. "I don't care what you say about me, but I'm done. I'm going to the police."

"We had a deal, David. You go to the police now, and it will be your word against Liv's. You have no proof of what she did to you. You're almost there."

"She's right, David," my mother says in the background.

"Four more days, David. You have to convince Liv you are nothing without her. Emily already laid it out for you. Just finish the work."

I shut the phone, wondering about Emily. How could she have fooled me?

There's a side to women I don't know, but this is part of my discovery. When this is all over, I hope I'm ten times wiser.

Day 26

Liv

I'm almost done with my thirty-day wisdom project, and I can't believe how much I've learned about people, but mostly about myself. Call me manipulative, but I must give myself a reward for being such a genius. I need to celebrate. After joining the search for David, I go on a shopping spree.

***

I leave my new clothes and shoes inside the garage then head inside, looking like I'm so exhausted. "I'm home."

David sits on the stairway, his chin resting on both hands.

"What a day. You'll be surprised how many people volunteered to look for you. There's even a hash tag trending on Twitter called

#SearchforDavid, and people are talking about doing a fundraiser."

His expression doesn't change one bit. "Have you ever thought how fucked up we both are?"

I join him by the stairs. "That's why we belong together."

"What is it you like about me?"

I brush my knees against his. "You're *you*."

"But you can have anyone you want."

I flash him a lopsided grin. "Why did you go with Emily?"

He wipes his mouth with the back of his hand. "You may be beautiful, successful, and smart..." he pauses to gather his breath. "but she made me feel special."

I release an exasperated sigh. "By fucking you and painting murals."

"That's something you'll never understand, Liv. You don't know how it feels to have someone love you for who you are, to feel oblivious to everything else."

"So why are you here? Why did you come home?"

"Because I don't want Emily to see me this way. I want her to remember the David I was to her."

Boy, this woman really cast a spell on my David. For the first time, I don't have the perfect response.

"I thought we rebuilt our connection these past few days, but I've come to realize the reason why I wanted to leave you in the first place," he says. "But it's okay. I only have a few days to live, and I don't want to die a bitter man."

I'm not sure if David is sincere and I don't understand the emotions I'm going through now. But all I can say is, "As you wish, David." Rising from the stairs, I stride to the bedroom and shut the door.

He's not the hero. I am.

Day 27

David

Liv tosses The San Francisco Chronicle on the countertop as I chew on my bagel. "Checkout page seven," she says with conviction.

I flip through the pages and stop as I spot Emily's face.

"'Emily Scott accepts seven-figure deal from Penguin to write her memoir, which features her life with David Walters,'" Liv reads the article title as if I can't. "I was so right."

I push the paper aside and take a sip of my orange juice.

"I have a meeting today with James Griffin. He's going to help me set up a David Walters' foundation fund."

I almost choke. "What?"

"What am I supposed to do with people who are donating money for our cause to help find you?"

I've lost my appetite and can't begin to comprehend how far Liv will take this.

"The fund will be used to help find missing people." She fixes her hair. "How do I look?"

My gaze sweeps over her black pin-stripe suit, and I give her a thumbs up. "Will you ever be going back to work, Liv?"

"Work?" She raises her eyebrows. "How can I work when I'm searching for my missing husband?" Liv heads for the door then comes back. "I need to let Detective Reed know by tomorrow you came home; otherwise, they won't stop hounding me."

"What? Why?"

"Because if we're going as planned, you have three days till you croak." She winks.

As she leaves, I pull the newspaper and trace Emily's face.

Women. Why do they have to be so complicated?

***

Liv removes her coat and heads for the dressing room as I lie in bed, glued to the TV. "Aren't you going to ask me how my day was?" she asks.

"My heart goes to the volunteers who contributed to The David Walters' Fund."

"Well." She kicks off her heels and slips on a nightie. "You'll be thrilled to know we've already raised a hundred thousand for this fund."

I feel sick to my stomach. What has my plan accomplished? Even if I get out of here, I won't be with Emily. What do I have to look forward to? "What are you supposed to do with this fund when you announce to the whole world I'm alive?"

She curls up on the bed and strokes my chest. "When you're gone, The David Walters Fund will be the legacy you leave behind."

My breathing grows rapid. Liv seems to have no remorse about me dying. She talks about it like we're planning our next meal.

"I know what you're thinking. Going on a shopping spree is the last thing on my mind. Although I'm a trustee for this foundation, there are a couple of other trustees who make the decisions too." She nibbles on my ear.

I just lie there, stiff like a log, hating every moment of my life.

Liv leaps on top of me and presses her lips to mine.

"You know I can't. I'm weak and don't have any urges."

"Really? Have you forgotten how strong you were when you pulled my hair?"

I turn to the other side, not looking forward to tomorrow.

"I want you to make love to me."

All I can do is release an exasperated sigh.

"Or shall I put it more blatantly? *I want you to fuck me.*"

She's playing with me, and I'll let her think that she has the upper hand. For now.

Day 27

Liv

I've managed to convince David to have sex and don't care if I did everything as he lay there, tired like a withered rose. I wanted to feel him inside me since I've forgotten how it felt to have sex with David after so long.

As we both release, I collapse beside him and hold David in a tight embrace. David is my husband. The whole world may be interested to hear Emily Scott's story, but she only shared a few moments with David. *I shared a whole lifetime with him.*

"We need to rehearse your homecoming story," I whisper.

"No need to sensationalize it, Liv," he grunts.

It's the story of a lifetime, like the prodigal son who returns home to his father. Everybody in America is rooting for David to come home to his beloved wife. I beam as heat emanates inside me. This will be a miracle of all miracles.

"Here's we'll tell them. A homeless man found you wandering about in *Crissy Fields*. You were attacked and robbed by a jogger who stole your watch and wallet, which explains your bloody shirt. You called me, and I picked you up and brought you home."

"Yay! We'll both get to be prom king and queen." He claps his hands and shakes his head. "Have you ever thought of writing a book? You're such a good storyteller. How many lies will it take you to finally face the truth, Liv?"

I ignore him. "Everyone including the press, will want to get a piece of you, but of course, I'll tell them you need to rest and we need our privacy."

He forces a nod.

"Don't you see, David? You'll come out a hero. You provide hope to every family who has lost a loved one. And I will be the happiest wife."

"Not for long." He faces me. "We still have a deal."

"I know, I know. You better get some rest. We have a big day tomorrow."

David doesn't realize this will actually be my reigning moment.

Day 28

David

I barely got any sleep last night. After Liv manipulating me into having sex with her and rehearsing her fabricated story, I can't wait till this is over. She belongs in jail.

Liv left for the hospital. She's going to talk to her boss about going back to work soon. The bills have been piling up, and she needs to act normal before my homecoming. I'm glad she leaves me alone, and I'm dying to get out of the house.

It's time I call Ruby.

She answers after one ring.

"Do you think I can at least see Emily today?" I ask her.

"How foolish can you be?" Ruby darts back. "Two more days, David, and it'll be over."

"I need to find out if Emily still loves me."

"Forget about Emily. Your emotions are going to cloud your vision. Rehearse what you need to say to the press and everyone who cares about your status."

"You sound just like Liv."

She passes the phone to my mother. "David, I miss you. Everything will be fine. You need to be patient."

Her words are comforting and encouraging, but deep inside, I know she's hurting.

"I miss you too, Mom. This will end soon, and we can put this behind us."

"Be strong, David," she cries. "I'll see you soon."

I can't take away the misery I've caused my mother, but I promise to make it up to her.

After I hang up, I hold the phone on my chest. Before I can move on with my life, I need to know the truth. I pace around the room, gathering the courage to call Emily. She answers after five rings.

"Emily," I breathe hard. "It's me."

All I hear is her heavy breathing.

"I'm still pushing through with my plan. Two more days. I need you to trust me."

"David, David, David. For a man who is older than me, you're quite idealistic."

I rub my chin, hoping she'll give me a chance. "Is it true you're writing a book?"

"I'm not obliged to tell you anything." Her tone is laced with sarcasm.

"You told Liv about our special moment at the skate park, when you showed me the mural and shared about your mom's death."

She chuckles. "Boy, your wife has you wrapped around her fingers. She's still your commander up until to the very end."

It's as if she kicked me in the stomach. I hate that she thinks I'm a loser. "I get it, Emily. I guess Liv was right. You used me to achieve fame, and someone as high and mighty like you doesn't want to be with me."

"Stop making this about me when you got me in this mess in the first place," she accuses.

From the sound of her voice, I can tell she still cares.

With head bowed, I lower my voice. "For what it's worth, I'm deeply sorry. I never wanted to hurt you. You probably think I'm a pathetic loser, but when this is done, you'll understand why I did it this way."

She doesn't say a word.

"Just so you're aware, tonight Liv will inform the press I'm home. Tomorrow we'll celebrate her birthday. The day after is when I will pursue my goal."

"What if everything goes wrong?"

"Failure is not an option." I share with her about the hidden cameras and Ruby's assistance.

"What time will you do this?"

"Eight at night. The cops and press will come... I hope you will be there."

A moment of silence crosses between us.

"I hope everything goes according to plan, but I must confess I can't be a part of it," she says.

Emily sniffs, and I wish she still felt the same about me. Even if we don't get back together, what matters is that we've made peace.

"I understand, Emily. I wish I met you in a different circumstance. I wish you the best."

Not waiting for her reply, I focus on moving forward. *Freedom is the only thing I yearn for now.*

Day 28

Liv

David is waiting by the stairs. The potassium chloride is ready, just need to store it in a safe place. I hang my coat on the rack and set the keys on the ring.

"How was work?" He folds his arms.

"Aside from the sympathetic stares from everyone, my boss agreed I can return soon."

"Good. You'll be better off without me, not to mention a wealthy woman with an objective."

I try to hide my grin, knowing I made use of my props, and it's time to rise above. David doesn't provide any use for me anymore. He served his purpose, and I don't want his disappearance to be overtaken by my status of being the good, martyr wife—the hero.

David follows me to the kitchen as we gear up to call the press.

David slips into soiled clothes and I smudge his face with mud from our backyard. His chin feels scruffy beneath my dirty fingers. David greases his hair with oil. I practice my tone of voice while David slaps my cheeks to make them flushed. Chopping onions helps me tear up. *Voila!* We're ready to do our charades for the media.

I make one quick call to Detective Reed, send a text to Chuck to gather his crew over, turn on the lights in every room, and have David lie down on the couch with a blanket.

There's a knock on the door.

Detective Reed wraps her oatmeal-colored sweater around her neck when she greets me. After drying my cheeks, I embrace her tight. "He's home. It's a miracle."

Her gaze scans the hallway before facing me in time for Chuck and his crew to arrive. She shakes her head. "I can't believe it. How did you hear?" she calls out to Chuck, who instructs his crew to bring in the lights.

"Do you mind?" He blocks her way and shakes my hand. "Hello, Liv. You must be so relieved David's home. Where is the lucky man?"

I escort them inside, and they peer into David's eyes. "He's still weak."

"You have to take him to the doctor. He might be dehydrated," Detective Reed says.

"I checked his vital signs. He's fine. He just needs to rest."

The cameraman focuses the camera on David then toward me while Chuck requests I sit beside David and relay to the whole world what occurred. Detective Reed listens intently.

Tucking a strand around my ear, I bow my head as tears stain my cheeks. "After I arrived from work today, I received a phone call from a man who said he believed he spotted David. He provided a description and told me to meet him at Crissy Fields." I dab my cheeks with a Kleenex. "At first, I thought this man was lying, but I still needed to check. Right when I saw him, I knew it was David."

"Did David say what happened?" Chuck asks.

"He's still having trouble remembering, but he recognizes me and his home." I squeeze David's knee.

"This is indeed a miracle that doesn't happen everyday. Olivia, did you honestly think David would return?"

I slowly lift my head and face the camera. "There were days I thought I could never survive, but I reminded myself of that four letter word *hope*. It's because of *hope* David returned. It's only through *hope* we prolong ourselves to keep going another day."

"You're such an inspiration to us."

Heat emanates in my cheeks as I smile widely. "I want to thank everyone who supported me during this time. I wouldn't have made it without you. Oh, and I almost forgot. Tomorrow is my birthday. This has been the best birthday gift ever. David came home for my birthday."

David blinks and smiles. To me, it looks forced, but hopefully no one else will notice.

"Wow! Happy Birthday! This indeed calls for a celebration. What's next for David and Olivia?"

"For now, we would like to request for our privacy as David regains his strength."

"Thank you, Olivia Walters." Chuck shifts toward the camera. "There you have it. David was lost and is now found, a powerful story of hope that shouldn't be forgotten. We hope to catch up again with the Walters couple next time."

The lights go off.

"You don't know how much you've boosted my career," Chuck says.

"You're welcome." I escort him out.

Detective Reed trails behind. "Something doesn't fit," she says, her gaze toward David.

"Let's just be happy David is home."

She shakes her head. "I'm going to try and sleep on it."

"Good night." I hold the door ajar.

I always have to win. Just wait for the surprise I have waiting. Two days from now, I will shock the world.

Olivia Walters will be a name you will hear among whispers, a name that will bear headlines, a name that will never be forgotten.

Day 29

David

Liv sets the table with matching balloons, her birthday cake, and the ribs and steak we just finished grilling.

"Let's dig in," she says with a twinkle in her eyes.

Although the phone doesn't stop ringing off the hook with reporters requesting interviews, I've never seen Liv so peaceful. She portrays an angelic face as we savor our food.

When we're almost done, I set a small box on the table and push it slowly toward Liv. "A present for you." I pretend to take ragged breaths.

Raising her eyebrows, she opens the box like a little kid when she receives a new toy. Flashing upon her is the silver watch she gave me back in college when we started dating, the very first gift she gave me. She stares at the watch like she's lost in space then affixes her gaze upon me with tear-filled eyes.

A moment of silence crosses between us, and it's only during this period do I feel that she truly loves me. Our gazes lock, and we rip off our clothes, the plates crashing onto the floor. She spreads her legs, and I'm thrusting inside her. I can't seem to control myself, and neither can she. We go on for a long time before releasing into ecstasy.

Liv pulls away and slips back into her dress while I zip my pants up. She slices two pieces of chocolate cake and serves me. Wiping sweat from my forehead, I devour the chocolate, a bit jolted by what just happened. I'm even more embarrassed now. The hidden camera. Ruby and my mother could have been watching.

What if what they say is true, that I'm connected to my psychotic wife one way or another? I can't seem to let go of her no matter what I do.

"I was supposed to sing Happy Birthday to you."

She slips the watch onto her wrist. "I guess we got carried away."

We share a laugh, and suddenly, it's just both of us again, obsessed with each other like how we used o be. How could this be happening? And why am I even enjoying this? *Am I psychopath too?*

Day 29

Liv

I feel like I'm nineteen again and very much in love. Did we just have sex? And David seems sentimental as ever to give me back his watch, the same one I bought him back in college. I had saved up all my tips from my waitressing job to get him that gift. He always valued it with his life.

What am I going to do when David is gone? Nobody can take his place. I know we've been through a rough patch, but every marriage encounters that. Although a part of me hates him, I can't live without him. Alone, we are two different souls hungry for attention, but together, we can be something. If only we can create the Olivia and David Walters recipe for success or the Olivia and David Walters thirty-day wisdom program.

I chuckle to myself. We are capable of creating beauty from ashes. Ever since he came home, he's glowing and it's all because of me. I am his potion, and I have taken care of him. I am a good wife. I am Olivia Walters. Nobody comes between David and me, not even his lies.

As we clear out the dishes, a knock startles us.

"Did you invite anyone?" David turns to me as I dry the utensils.

"It's probably those damn reporters."

David wipes his hand on the kitchen towel and heads to the front door. I follow from behind.

The knocks grow louder and David takes a peek on the peephole. Without asking me, he opens the door wide. Christopher and Patrick march in with a bottle of wine and a gift bag.

"Look who we have here." David hugs Christopher and shakes Patrick's hand.

"Couldn't miss your birthday," Christopher says to me. "David, it's a miracle. You look amazing."

David blushes and shuts the door. "Thank you."

"This is Patrick."

Patrick shakes our hands but doesn't look at me.

Christopher leads the way to the living room. "Where's the party?"

A creepy sensation rolls up my back. Why did David have to open the door? "We just finished dinner. Would you like some cake?"

"Cake it is." Christopher and Patrick settle onto the couch. David sits beside them.

I take the wine to the kitchen and cut two slices of cake. *Fuck!* This was supposed to be my night with David.

After I trail back to the living room, I hand them their slices of cake.

"Liv you're so famous now. Your face is on every channel. That's probably why you don't call me anymore," Christopher says.

A forced smile plays on my lips. "Been making up for lost time."

"Or could it be guilt from what you did while you were on the cruise and after," Patrick adds.

I clear my throat. "Do you guys want some more cake?"

"You heard me." Patrick eyes David. "Do you know what your wife did?"

"Patrick, this isn't the time and place." Christopher waves his hand in the air.

Patrick leans forward. "While you were in your own world, David, your wife was screwing this man Aiden. In fact, when you escaped, they did it in your bedroom."

"Stop it," Christopher yells.

"But what I find disturbing is that he dies of a heart attack while having sex. She calls Christopher to cover up for her because she doesn't want people to know she was a philandering wife."

Although David is aware of my affair, I assume he doesn't know I killed Aiden. My body is frozen, and I can't look at David.

"Don't you find that strange? Two men. One suffers from a coma, and the other one a heart attack."

David stands from the couch. "Patrick, it was nice meeting you, but you should leave now."

Christopher tugs Patrick and whispers, "I'm sorry."

I'm still appalled by what's happening, but more than anything, I'm proud of how my husband handled it. He is my man, and all the more I'm convinced we belong together. We don't need anything else when we have each other.

"Gladly." Patrick tosses the gift bag to me. "I hope you enjoy your birthday."

David and I stand in silence as they leave. I don't know what to say to him. I've committed crimes because of the one man I can't live without.

He pulls me toward him and embraces me. How I wish this moment could stop. How I long for more days like these with David. I love being his wife. I will never take him for granted again.

But these demons will never stop haunting me. David and I will never have a peaceful life again. So much has been done.

It has to end tomorrow.

Day 30

David

I wake up all fuzzy from a deep sleep. Reaching my hand on the sheets, I check to see if Liv is there, but she's gone. Today is the day. Do I actually know what I've gotten myself into? Can I possibly push through with my plan? I counted the days till it would come, but now that it's here, I feel like a groom having cold feet.

Whoever invented time anyway? Why can't we just exist in between time and space? Perhaps they can just freeze my body and I can wake up and everything will still be the same.

"Liv," I call out to her as I head to the bathroom. She's not there so I dash downstairs. There's no sign of her except for a note on the counter.

David,

I went for a hike. Meet me at Golden Gate Bridge around noon.
Love,
Liv

An hour and a half yet. Why would she want to meet at the Golden Gate Bridge? Then it dawns on me. The bridge was where I proposed. The twinkle in her eye remains etched on my memory. Liv must want to spend our last moments here.

I run up the stairs, stride to my office, and remove the disposable phone from underneath my desk.

Ruby picks up. "David, I've been waiting for your call. Will you be doing this at eight o'clock as promised?"

My palms sweat, and I can't answer.

"David, you've waited for this day. There's no way you're backing out now."

Women! They always have strong intuition.

"David, I know what you're thinking. Have you forgotten what Liv did to you? Do you want to remain her prisoner?"

Gripping the phone, I straighten my shoulders. "I'm tired of people telling me what to do. If it's not Liv, it's you. I'm going to do this my way." After I hang up the phone, I pull out all the hidden cameras and store them inside our closet. I jump into the shower and get dressed. It's time I tell Liv we'll start somewhere new, where nobody knows us. But should I? I don't know why I feel this way, but after all we've been through, Liv seems to be there for me. We were once very much in love. A second chance is all we need.

***

The sun is immaculate as tourists flock to the Golden Gate Bridge. If the bridge could speak, it would have many stories to tell. Our story will change tonight, *if* I push through with my plan. Ruby will make one phone call to Detective Reed, who will lock Liv up, and I can live as a free man.

Liv didn't tell me where exactly we should meet, but I know she'll be waiting for me right at the center. I still have fifteen minutes before noon, but I'm glad I arrive early.

I spot her hair shining against the sun. Her red scarf brightens her face as she leans back on the railings. I wave slowly approaching her. "Liv."

She stares at me blankly, like she doesn't recognize who I am.

"Liv."

Her lips form a line. "My name is not Liv. *I'm Red.*"

Is she playing another game? "Hello, Red. I'm David, your husband, remember?"

She studies me for a moment then affixes her gaze on the view. "My husband proposed to me here."

Crazy as it may sound, I like the way she refers to me in third person so I play along with her. There's nobody like Liv. "He must be a lucky man to have you."

She keeps her eyes glued to the water. "I wasn't a good wife. I did crazy stuff."

"Marriage isn't easy."

"I couldn't give him a child." A tear stains her cheek.

"Not everybody has children. We have a cute cat."

"I did bad things to him. Things a normal person wouldn't do."

I put my arm around her and whisper, "We can start over and forget about what happened. Go somewhere new."

I know for sure this is what I want. Perhaps we can make it work. We can forget and leave the past behind. She looks beautiful and fragile like when I first met her. That's it! I need to protect her again, to bring that beautiful smile back. The one she lost years ago.

Her breathing becomes more rapid. "My husband is dying. He has a brain tumor. Today is his last day."

"No, he's not. I lied to you."

She doesn't face me. "I can't bear to see him die. It wasn't his fault."

"You won't have to go through that. I told you I was lying to you." I point to my chest. "Look at me, Liv. I'm healthy and strong."

Glancing at me, she blinks. Her eyes look empty. "Why do you keep calling me Liv? My name is Red. Who are you?"

I take a step back. "Liv, it's me, David, your husband. Didn't you tell me to meet you here at the Golden Gate Bridge?"

Her eyebrows furrow, and she scratches her head. "He doesn't deserve me." She glances at the watch I gave her, removes it, and hands it to me. "Please give this to him."

I cling to the watch like it's a lifeline to her.

She closes her eyes. "It's time."

"Liv, you need to get a grip on yourself." I shake her. From the corner of my eye, I spot my mother, Ruby, and Detective Reed approaching the entrance of the bridge. Fuck! "We need to get out of here."

Liv opens her eyes and stares up at the sky, the sun glaring directly at her. "Please tell my husband I'm sorry, I wasn't the wife he deserved to have, and my only wish is to be happy."

With both hands, she pulls herself up the railings and takes a big leap, her arms swaying like an eagle.

I extend my arms, hoping to save her, but all I'm able to grab is her red scarf. Her body falls to the water and crashes through the waves. "Liv. Liv!"

Tourists yell behind me and cover their mouths. Ruby, Mom, and the detective rush to my side. A crowd of sea gulls flock to the water. People step out from their cars to see what happened but all I can do is yell again. *How could she do this to me?*

Moments later, I'm still astounded by what Liv did. I never expected her to do that, but now I realize it was *Liv's way*. She died to save me from her. Even in death, Liv pulled one over me. Even in death, Liv had to make a dramatic scene. Even in death, Liv wanted to depart from this world as not forgotten. Everybody will remember Olivia Walters as the woman who jumped off the Golden Gate Bridge. Liv beat me to it because she thought I was going to leave her again. *In the end, my wife, Olivia Walters wanted me to know she would die for me so I could be free.*

Day 30

Liv

David is a fool to believe I bought the story that he's dying. I've never seen him so strong and vibrant. I've accepted his choice. David doesn't love me. I can't force him to stay nor can I coerce him to love me. But I can do something more powerful. David will always remember me.

I wait for him at the Golden Gate Bridge. He will come. How can he not? I want to see him for the last time, the happy cheerful man he now is.

Gripping the red scarf I used the first night I met Aiden, I realize that choosing to forget I was David's wife and embracing my alter ego, Red, is the only way to erase the pain.

I never realized how symbolic this scarf has become. When you pretend you're someone else, it erases the pain you possess, the same pain I want to very much forget.

David waves at me from afar. He exposed the same boyish grin he had when I met him. But there's no time to think of that now.

Looking into David's eyes, I learn I can never make him happy again, but as I decide to depart from this world, there is one thing I will leave with David, a piece of me. *David will never forget me.*

As I take one last look at my husband, David and return the watch he gave me, I realize that I've completed my thirty-day project and this is the end. My goal is to remember the expression of the man I've truly loved before I lift myself up and jump. I'm now ready to make a big statement. Right when my body glides to the ocean, for the first time in my life, I've learned to let go. An image of flames flashes upon me, and I hear my foster parents screaming for help. I read the doctor's lips saying, "I'm sorry for the loss of your baby." I spot my husband's face on the first day I met him. Emily's mural and Aiden's face appears next. Everything that has haunted me will now end. Soon, peace surges inside me. There's no looking back. I close my eyes, and my body crashes to the waves.

"David!" I shout, air escaping my lungs moments before my head explodes on the rocks.

I'm now part of the ocean, never ending, never beginning, never forgotten.

Epilogue

Today marks one year since Liv died. I can still hear the echo as she yelled my name before her body crashed into the waves. I sometimes wonder if Liv thought this was a game where she could win or if this was part of her thirty-day wisdom project, but I'll never know. Although I don't live in San Francisco anymore, people still recognize me as the husband of the woman who jumped off the Golden Gate Bridge. Liv did a good job leaving her remnants behind.

I recently moved into a new condo in Seattle after living with Mom in Boston for eight months. She was afraid to let me live alone after what happened. As for Ruby, she felt justice was never served for her brother, Aiden. And Christopher and Patrick never anticipated Liv would do such a thing. It just goes to show that nobody, including me, knew what Liv was capable off. I completely forgot Liv set up *The David Walters* foundation. When they asked if I wanted to be a part of it, to help other missing people, I told them my desire of leaving everything behind.

Seattle is a great place to start over. Wilma, my cat and constant companion, provides comfort in the stillness of the night. Looks like I'll never be ready for a relationship. My work dynamics has changed. I have an office in the heart of the city and have a team of graphic designers working for me.

While I never heard from Emily again, I know she made a lot of money when she released her Memoir. However, it was a pale comparison to the news of Liv's death. There's no interest in my part to read the book. I often wonder what would have happened if Liv didn't end her life. Where would we be now?

I've found a surprising new hobby—skateboarding. That's right. Sometimes you need to get out of your comfort zone. Skating is very soothing, and although I'm probably one of the older guys here, I've challenged myself to swerve down the slopes with my new friends. At times, I find myself admiring a mural of fishes with different colors. Being a part of a skateboard club can be liberating. Nobody cares what I'm thinking, and they're not here to judge you.

Tonight, the group gathers together in a circle while the bonfire cackles. Jeremy, the leader of our skateboard club, suggests we get rid of the things that bind us. Tommy, the man sitting beside me, ditches his Zippo lighter as he professes that he'll quit smoking. Sitting across me, Arnold hurls his sets of dice, confessing how gambling hurt his family.

It's my turn. Rising from the stool, I toss Liv's red scarf into the roaring fire. The flames eagerly devour it, destroying the material, turning it even redder before it burns away, melting to ashes as I let go of the ghosts of my past. Tears spill from my cheeks as I release a breath, something I haven't done in a long time.

Tomorrow is a new day, and for once, I can live again.

Acknowledgements

A big thanks to my editors, Nicole Zoltack and Marcie Stevens for helping me shape my story. To my proofreader, Gail Picado, thanks for your keen eye and thorough work. To my formatter, Rachelle Ayala, thanks for always being so patient and helpful. Thanks to my cover artist, Natasha Brown for creating covers that are heartfelt and meaningful. Thanks to Angie Velez, Luisa Miciano and Bryanne Taladua for assisting me with my medical research. A big thanks to my loving husband, Arnel Solon, and sweet son, Stefan Solon, for your patience and understanding as I completed this novel. Thank you to all my readers and fans for supporting me with my books. Thank you to God for planting dreams and making them realities.

About the Author

Geraldine Solon is the award-winning, bestselling author of Love Letters, Chocolicious, The Assignment, The Lost Flower, Never Look Back, Thirty Days of Red and a marketing guidebook for authors, Authorpreneur in Pajamas. She served as Treasurer, Event Coordinator and Vice President for the Fremont Area Writers club. Geraldine lives in the San Francisco Bay area. www.geraldinesolon.com

Other Books by Geraldine